ARCHIPELAGO

ARCHIPELAGO

DAVID WARD

Red Deer
PRESS

Published in the United States in 2009

5 4 3 2 1

PUBLISHED BY
Red Deer Press
A Fitzhenry & Whiteside Company
www.reddeerpress.com

CREDITS
Edited by Peter Carver
Cover design and text design by Jacquie Morris & Delta Embree
Printed and bound in Canada

ACKNOWLEDGMENTS
Financial support provided by the Canada Council, and the Government of Canada through the Book Publishing Industry Development Program (BPIDP).

Canada Council for the Arts Conseil des Arts du Canada

Library and Archives Canada Cataloguing in Publication

Ward, David, 1967-
Archipelago / David Ward.

ISBN 978-0-88995-400-7

I. Title.

PS8595.A69A73 2008 jC813'.6 C2008-903794-4

Publisher Cataloging-in-Publication Data (U.S)

Ward, David, 1967-

Archipelago / David Ward.

[196] p. : cm.

Summary: Twelve-year-old Jonah and his mother are on a self-healing mission after the loss of his father. Living in the Queen Charlotte Islands, Jonah sees a mysterious girl appear wading in the waters, and even more mysterious is the mist that saves Jonah after falling off a cliff, plunging him back in time 14,000 years.

ISBN: 978-0-88995-400-7 (pbk.)

1. Time travel — Juvenile fiction. 2. Fantasy. I. Title.

[Fic] dc22 PZ7.W373Arc 2008

ANCIENT FOREST FRIENDLY

25 trees were saved for our forests

Preserving our environment

Red Deer Press chose to use recycled paper to print this book and saved these resources[1]:

energy	water	greenhouse gases	solid waste
17 million BTUs	34,487 L	996 kg	531 kg

Printed by **Webcom Inc.** on Legacy Offset 100% post-consumer waste.

Recycled
Supporting responsible use of forest resources

Cert no. SW-COC-002358
www.fsc.org
© 1996 Forest Stewardship Council

[1]Estimates were made using the Environmental Defense Paper Calculator.

ACKNOWLEDGMENTS

I would like to thank Renee Hetherington, Paul Tigchelaar, and Michelle Davis for their contributions to this book. Paul's antics during our kayak trip through Haida Gwaii provided so many stimulants for the plot. Renee, thank you for your time and research contributions and for clarifying correct flora and fauna of the ancient environment. Michelle, your primary editing was exceptional. I would also like to thank my editor Peter Carver for guiding and shaping this story with conscientious precision. And, finally, my agent, Scott Treimel, for your belief in and pursuit of this story. My thanks to you all.

Dedication

For

Steven Dreger,

Dan Heavenor,

David Wu,

Phil Ward,

Paul Kapular

and Troy Joshi,

my dearest friends

in life adventures.

Chapter One

From the cliff top, Jonah squinted at the glare off the sea. He was transfixed by a figure in the water nearly a kilometer away and thirty meters below. A girl waded in the shallows with the surf lapping against her knees. She reached down with her palms open to the surface as if to help steady her on an unbalanced floor. It was impossible to tell her age, and with his mother holding the binoculars, the best he could do was imagine.

He checked the beach, but the distance was too great to see any footprints. There did not seem to be anyone else around. He wanted to see her face. Not far from where she waded, a mist formed and its twisting tentacles reached ever closer to the shore. Jonah kept watch on its progress, waiting for it to encompass the girl and block her from sight.

A shadow flickered, and the sound of his mother's boots shifting on loose pebbles disturbed the rhythm of the sea. His mother would laugh at him for sure. She always did when he glanced at girls. Her shadow washed over him and disappeared over the cliff. Jonah wished the girl into hiding behind the outcrop where his own kayak was sheltered.

His mother checked her watch. Almost time to head down. She raised the binoculars and aimed at the beach below.

Jonah waited for her to comment. When she said nothing, he glanced up. How could she have missed the girl? He frowned.

Their common silences had been irksome of late and growing more frequent by the day. Perhaps the girl was a welcome distraction. It would give them something to talk about.

He leaned closer to the edge and forced his eyes open against the breeze. The girl was young, at least in the right age range, maybe thirteen at the most. He caught the gleam of her dark hair.

"What are you looking at?" his mother asked suddenly. She leaned over him to pan the water.

"Uh . . . down there."

He followed her gaze past the beach to the next headland and to the open sea. The islands of the Queen Charlottes lay dotted to the horizon as if sown carelessly by a goddess of the deep. Jonah smiled at the analogy. His mother wouldn't get it. His smile faded. His father might have. It was another example of their differences. His father had hungered after the larger questions of life, the world, and God. His mother did not. She was practical and reliable. Jonah often found himself living in the spaces between his parents.

Some of the islands lay low with their salt-stained stone shores hugging the water while others thrust cedars and hemlocks to the sky, as if each were competing with the rest for a better view of the world. It was a wild, lonely part of the universe. The Haida Nation called it *Haida Gwaii*—"the islands of the people." There did not appear to be many people here anymore.

His mother straightened. "You're looking at something. What is it?"

He pointed vaguely to the beach and to the water.

She watched his waving finger. "Are you bored? Want to head back down? I've shot everything I need to from here."

How could she not see the girl? Above the rumble of the tide, his mother's binoculars clanked against the rest of her camera equipment.

She looked up. "Well?"

"Can I have those for a second?" The eye pieces were cold against his skin.

"What for, Hawkeye?"

He swept the beach. "Thought I saw something."

"Jonah?"

He frowned. Every time there was something worth looking at with binoculars, he couldn't find it. "Okay. Let's go."

He stood quickly, too quickly, and slid on the loose gravel. Scrambling to save the binoculars, his feet shot out from under him and he landed on his stomach. A shower of stones went over the cliff. He dug his fingers into the gravel and slammed his cheek into the ground. He slid another six inches, gravity now working against him.

Thirty meters. His father had fallen thirty meters.

His chin slid into open space. Ocean waves rolled over jagged rocks, like old bones stirred in a pot; they rose and fell with the brine. He was going over.

"Mom!" His voice caught in his throat as a strangled whisper. "Help!"

Mist suddenly appeared below as if summoned by his cry, small as a cloud, the size of a sheep, moving toward him. It rose swiftly, gaining speed and size. Soon it was as big as a whale, expanding against the rock face. His eyes widened at its approach, but there was nothing he could do. Cool, dense air swelled beneath him as the mist drew closer.

His shoulders were now over the edge, and the shock of emptiness made him dizzy. It was only a moment before he would tip into the void and begin the fatal rush to the bottom. But the mist came faster. When it struck, it blew him backwards with the force of a geyser, landing him safely, although roughly, onto solid ground.

"Hey! What are you doing?" His mother grabbed him. He felt the blood draining from his face, felt sick to his stomach. He stared over her shoulder but the cloud was gone.

She pulled him close. "Are you crazy? What were you doing? What were you thinking?"

He looked up, searching the sky for the mist.

She held his chin. "Don't do that again. Ever again!" She squeezed him tightly. "I didn't bring you along to fall off a cliff for the sake of binoculars. You've got to be smarter than that, Jonah." She closed her eyes and bowed her head. "One was enough."

With his heart still pounding, he pulled away. "Did you see that, Mom? It came when I called."

She inhaled deeply, trying to get her breath. "You're too much like your father. You're too young, too careless for a place like this."

Hot anger brought the blood back to his cheeks. Six months ago he could have handled a comment like that. But six months ago his father had been alive. He tore his eyes away from the sky and picked up the binoculars. "I'm twelve! I sat up too fast and got a little dizzy. You didn't even see what happened." He rolled onto his side. "And you did not *bring* me on this trip. I volunteered. Don't forget who remembered to put the food up in the cache when you drifted off last night. And it was me who cranked our water this morning even though *you* didn't clean the pump last night, either. I'm not crazy. And I'm not too careless." What he did not say was that losing one parent had made him mortally afraid of losing the other.

She pursed her lips thoughtfully. "No. You're not crazy. But stay away from cliff edges. Do you hear me? Do you get that? For both our sakes."

Jonah waited for the life to return to his legs and the whirligigs to clear from his sight. It had happened so quickly. "I didn't mean to get so close."

His mother's hands shook. She stuffed them in her pockets.

He peered over the hungry ocean, keeping his feet firmly planted. Not a hint of mist anywhere. "Weird," he whispered. The taste of salt and spray from the rocks revived him. "Lucky gust." Yet even as he spoke the words, he knew it wasn't true. "It's almost like it came when I called." He clenched and unclenched his hands. His knees and fingers were a little torn up from grabbing at the gravel, but that was all. He had taken far worse in a soccer game.

The girl moved gracefully as before through an ocean she shared with no one. The terror of the cliff top lessened.

"Hey, Mom? Did you see a fog patch down there?"

"There hasn't been any fog for days." Her voice was tense.

The girl turned to face the beach. Jonah set his hands on his hips. "Did we pass anyone on the way here?"

"On the way where?"

"Into De la Beche."

She shook her head. "I don't remember seeing anything or anyone since we entered the park. But this won't work, Jonah. I'm still mad at you. I'm not sure you understand. Out here, you can be seriously injured in a second. Certain things have to change in this family."

Jonah snorted. "You mean *you* and *me*. I get it. I'll never take another risk so that I don't die like Dad!"

His mother squeezed her eyes shut.

Jonah cringed. After a long silence he said, "Sorry. It popped out. I'm changing the subject. What about that sailboat? When did we see that? Yesterday? It could have been making for the bay."

Without opening her eyes, she answered, "Jonah, what does it matter?"

"Thought I saw someone down there. Did you?"

His mother took a deep breath, then reached for her backpack.

"No. And I doubt the boat was coming here. There isn't much reason to come to De la Beche. Most people head to Hot Spring Island as soon as possible. Good thing. I didn't come here to photograph people."

The West Coast Diving Society had given permission to his mother, Maggie Townend, the famous travel photographer, to use a float house on the eastern portion of the bay as a base. It was a favor not granted to many. Although the bunks were reserved for divers, it was still a dry place to store over a hundred pounds of camera equipment and film. But he preferred the beach. By the second night of sleeping on the ground, they were accustomed to life in a musty tent.

His mother was on an exhaustive photo-shoot in Gwaii Haanas, the South Moresby National Park, and he knew to expect more discomfort ahead. An image of the cliff and the swirling water shot through his head. There was no water where his father had fallen. Only rocks. No mercy. *Think about the girl; think about fishing.*

He took the pack from his mother and slung it easily over his shoulders. His sweaty shirt slid across his back. He drew even with her. "Could we camp on the beach tonight?"

She shrugged.

"I want to fish until dark and there's a casting rock at the headland." If they hurried, the girl might still be in the water. Perhaps, too, he could see where the mist had come from.

"Fine. But you're going to have to do it on your own." She softened the reproach. "I have to change lenses, check the route for tomorrow, and call the office. I also need a couple of hours on the float, waterproofing and choosing my gear."

Jonah tapped her arm. "Your hands are shaking."

"Well, you scared the crap out of me!"

"I know! I scared me, too." He grabbed her pack as she turned away. "Don't worry so much." Their eyes met. "Don't worry so much," he repeated. "The trip just started. I'll be okay."

She raised her eyebrows. "We're heading to the Bischofs group at dawn." Then she glanced at the cliff top, at Jonah, and turned for the woods.

He grinned triumphantly. The cliff was behind him and a mystery ahead.

The Bischofs were a strange troop of islands, seemingly cut adrift from the rest of the archipelago. He had been curious back in the city and by now, so close, he could hardly wait. Hot Spring Island was a highlight of the Charlottes as well, and boaters came from everywhere to soak in the natural "hot tubs." As for the Dolomite Narrows, it was the greatest zone of marine life on the West Coast. His fishing rod was ready.

"I can move everything, set it up, and still have a fish sizzling by five."

She looked relieved, though he couldn't tell whether it was from the change of topic or the fact that he was still alive. "I'd like that," she said. "Are you ready?"

"Yep."

The moment they entered the woods, the light dimmed and they slowed while their eyes adjusted. The trees were enormous, and leafy foliage blotted out any trace of the sky. Shifting patterns fell across the ferns at their feet, and the smell of steaming earth rose wherever the light touched.

Jonah sniffed. There was an odd feeling to these woods—an ancient stuffiness that lingered amongst the gnarled trunks. Moss covered everything. Sheets of green and mottled brown wrapped the trees like woolen fleece and flowed over the fallen timber.

His feet sank into the spongy ground and he watched his prints rise back up in the moss. He shivered. There was no trace of another human ever being here; if they had, they belonged to a different era.

Jonah looked at his footprints. *Fourteen thousand years!* In his mind, he saw a grunting figure, with low swinging arms. *Fourteen thousand years.* His mother's books and charts were strewn over the dining room table, and he had pored over them night after night while they were still in Vancouver. He imagined himself traveling across the ancient ice bridges from Asia and into Alaska, not knowing what he was going to find or if he could even survive. He could relate to people like that; wandering, searching, always living with the unknown. He shared those feelings these days. And the fear that came with it.

He sighed. It was an undiscovered country, a place for adventures. And God knew he needed one of those! An adventure. A quest. Something that at its end would be a clue as to how he could possibly carry on without his father. "That's what I want!" he murmured. "A quest. Right time. Right place." He glanced up and said, "Hear that? I want a quest. You took my dad. The least you could do is give me some direction." He felt a little strange. "What am I doing?" he muttered, suddenly disgusted with himself for praying. "Waste of time."

The words had hardly left his lips when a gust of wind rushed through the trees, sending the branches swaying and dipping. His eyes wide, Jonah ran to catch up to his mother.

The maps he looked at had shown that some of the ancient adventurers had worked their way south through the Canadian interior, while some continued into what are now the rainforests of British Columbia. Some went even further, to California and South America. His heart thumped. What an adventure! Anything could happen. He squared his shoulders. Ancient adventurers had to keep their eyes open and their wits about them!

A spider's web caught him full in the mouth and he sputtered. He pulled away, only to thrust into another, larger web. Jonah flapped his arms about his head. He stepped blindly into a tree.

"Use a stick . . . out in front of you!" his mother said.

"It's kind of thick through here," he said. "This isn't the way we came up, is it?" He started whistling.

"I have no idea. But we're not lost or anything," she added. "I mean, it's an island. We just head down to the water, then follow the beach back to the boats. Can you *please* not whistle?"

She touched the map sticking out of her shorts and Jonah smiled at the gesture. She lived by maps—in more ways than one. "It would help if we could find that stream we followed on the way up," she muttered. His own map remained in his pocket. She insisted he have one at the start of every trip, but he never took it out until the ride home.

His mother stopped. He stepped beside her and stared down the embankment. The ground dropped quickly, breaking into undulating plateaus as if an avalanche had rumbled through. "*That* is not the way we came." He pointed.

"Shhh!" She motioned him to silence.

They strained to hear between the rustling of branches and swishing treetops. A moment later she tapped her shorts pocket. "Told you."

The sound of rushing water grew louder and a clean, cool breeze announced it. The air, pushed up by the tumbling stream, defeated the black flies that had followed them through the woods. The stream bed cut into the hill and they scrambled down onto the gravel. Tree branches hung far out over the water and enormous roots burst through the eroding embankment like thirsty worms.

"Don't get your . . ."

He stepped high to avoid a stone and his foot landed in the water.

"... feet wet," his mother finished. She rolled her eyes. "His father's son," she muttered.

"What did you say?"

"Nothing!"

Jonah shook freezing water from his boot. The chill was shocking and he was half tempted to untie his boot and beat his toes back to life. The Charlottes were a conundrum. Of all his mother's expeditions, there never had been a more beautiful place, or one less forgiving to its visitors. It was good discussion for the fireside—that, and the oddity of the mist. Ordinarily it was a conversation he would have had with his father. One thing he was certain his dad would have agreed with: the mist had not been a lucky gust.

Then he smirked. Maybe there would be more to tell his mom about a girl, as well. For a quiet place, a lot had happened already. The trees looked on indifferently while the stream lunged hungrily for Jonah's other boot.

A patch of brightness found its way through the trees ahead, promising a clear path to the beach. The sound of waves hitting the shore overtook the tumbling stream, and a gentle wind worked its way around his mother, whipping his face teasingly.

"You're whistling again," she muttered.

"I remember this," he said.

"Me too. I think the stream was choked ahead, right? That's why we didn't start in the stream until farther ahead. We should climb out of the creek bed soon."

Staring at the congestion of trunks and boulders filling the creek, Jonah pointed. "I think we can make it." He stepped past his mother toward the light.

"Freeze!" she yelled.

CHAPTER TWO

ICY WATER FLOWED OVER HIS BOOTS. HIS MOTHER AIMED HER CAMERA.

"Perfect shot. You're caught like a shadow and all the branches are sticking out of you. Fabulous! Front cover stuff."

He could hear clicking as she moved toward him, angling her body to take in the sky, the forest, and the glimmering stream. With her baseball cap extended over the lens, and the light dazzling his eyes, she looked like some mythical creature.

"I thought you weren't going to film people." He held his balance, trying not to move. "Just nature."

"*You* are not *people*."

"You're standing in the water," he observed.

She stopped shooting. She lifted a foot. "So I am."

"Cold, isn't it?" he said.

"Yep."

The shore was deserted except for a pair of seagulls combing the sand with their sharp beaks. Jonah let the pack sink to the sand.

His mother walked to the water's edge and splashed her face. "Much better," she sighed. She pulled out a lens and sifted through her camera bag.

"I'm going to check the boats." Jonah said. "And the beach on the other side of that outcrop. Might be a better spot for the tent . . . or fish!"

She nodded. "Might be." She grabbed his pack. "Leave this with me. I'm going to the float soon. You'll be on your own for a bit and I want you where I can see you. So get the wandering feet out of your system now."

"It's a hundred meters away. I could paddle to it in two minutes."

"And a bear can kill in less than fifteen seconds." She smiled from behind her camera. "I'll be heading out in ten minutes. Be back by then."

Jonah pulled a face and pressed his nose up close to the lens. "There. Put that in your article!" He grinned.

"Ten minutes!" she warned. She took the picture. He walked like a monkey all the way to the giant outcrop of stone, enjoying her laughter. Happiness was foreign to them these days without his father, but somehow the wildness of the place allowed for the laughter with no loss of reverence.

Closer to the wall, he stopped acting and stared. It was unlikely the girl would have attempted the treacherous eight-meter outcrop in bare feet. Still, it was worth a look. Maybe she had swum around the rocks or gone back through the woods.

The stone was covered in green slime. Each handhold had to be carefully chosen to avoid the flesh-eating barnacles above the water line. But Jonah was a good climber. The skill ran in his blood and he felt the exhilaration that accompanies height. At the top, he turned to locate his mother. She looked tiny, wandering back to the kayaks. Her cameras bounced at her side, lenses, filters, and light meters flashing in the sun.

Ahead, De la Beche Inlet was buffered by a small island, keeping the open sea a perfect secret. Behind the trees lay the Bischof Islands, their next stop.

The beach was empty and no footprints disturbed the sand. He sighed, shaking his head. He began the descent backward, as one would go down a ladder, planting his boots on any ledge he could find while his fingers searched for handholds. The familiar feel of the rock made him look up. Ordinarily, his father would have been looking down at him, smiling and calling out instructions. Their best conversations happened when they went rock climbing. Hockey, girls, anything and everything. Now that his father's voice was silent, he longed for it all the more. His own thoughts felt quiet these days, a little empty and alone. It was as if God had fallen off the cliff as well.

He looked down between his boots. There was only about two meters to go and he decided to jump. Below, a cliff face jutted. He would have to push out hard not to skewer himself. He shifted his weight and jumped.

The push was not enough. His chest struck first, followed instantly by his forehead, and he bounced away from the wall violently.

He ended up on his backside with his fingers dug into the sand like a wayward ship dragging its anchor. His forehead screamed for attention, and he gasped when his fingers returned covered in blood. He looked up dizzily. The mist swirled off the water and twisted past him toward the trees. "It's back," he whispered.

The ocean crashed ferociously. His stomach churned, and no matter how hard he resisted, a tear squeezed out. For the briefest moment he wanted his mother. He gritted his teeth and brushed away the tear. *I can do this.*

When everything stopped swirling, he let out a breath and slumped. Just at the edge of his vision, he caught a glimpse of something, a presence directly behind him. His chin shot up.
He threw himself forward and away, turning in the air to face his attacker. The mist continued to swirl and he strained to see through

it. *Teeth . . . body . . . eyes.* Standing no more than two meters away was a pair of sand-spattered bare legs. They belonged to a girl.

He shook his head and swiped his eyes. Long, black hair hung over the girl's shoulders. He dropped his stare.

"I'm sorry, I didn't . . . I mean . . ." He regarded her toes. Her feet were tanned brown like the rest of her body. White salt lines circled her ankles. He watched her toes crinkle as she crouched, her arms tensed on either side as if ready to spring away. She was not naked, as he had first thought. A smooth cloth, a towel perhaps, soaked by the ocean and almost the same color as her face, clung to her like skin. At her waist, a thin leather belt held the cloth in place.

His eyes widened. In her hand she carried a stone the size of a fist. Her arm was drawn back ready to strike.

"Wait! Don't!" he yelled.

Jonah peered up through his fingers and into a pair of large brown eyes. Quick as a cat, she turned, expertly balanced, so that she could see both the heights and the woods behind him.

"Could you put the rock down? I'm not going to do anything." He started to sit up but the girl raised her arm higher and narrowed her eyes. He could see she knew how to throw, and at that distance not even his mother could miss. They stared, silent, while around them the echo of the surf roared off the cliff.

"Do you speak English?" he asked, sitting straighter.

His movement startled her. She opened her eyes wide, flared her nostrils, and made herself bigger by extending her arms and legs. "Yaaaaaaaa!" she roared. She flicked her wrist as if to throw.

It was the strangest thing Jonah had ever seen a girl do in his life. He instinctively sank low. He had a vague memory of doing the same thing when a neighbor's dog once threatened him. The girl began to hiss at him.

"It's okay," he murmured. "Everything's okay."

The girl grunted with satisfaction. Her eyes roved from his hair to his boots and he could tell she was sizing him up. Apparently they were mutually surprised, for her eyes lingered on his hiking boots and buttoned shirt.

Jonah looked up. The girl stared back. Her eyes were still wide but she was squatting again. She was quite pretty in a wild sort of way. "My mom is back there," he stammered stupidly.

She stared at his lips, then, startled, glanced over his head to the rocky outcrop. She watched suspiciously.

"So you do understand," he murmured.

She scowled.

He scowled back. She wasn't like any girl at school. One of his best friends, Shonika, would have laughed at the skin-thing the girl was wearing. But not even Shonika would say anything with a rock pointed at her head.

And then the strangest thing happened. When the girl spoke, Jonah discovered that, while the words did not appear to be English, he could still understand them. Quite distinctly she said, "I cannot smell her."

Jonah blinked. Quite outside the fact that something confounding was happening to their speech, her comment was just as bewildering. With his heart beating rapidly, he croaked, "Smell who?"

The girl paused as if waiting for his words to translate as they do on international radio reports. She looked even more alarmed than he felt. "Your mother," she said. "There is no scent." Then she added, "Something strange is happening with our talking."

Her voice was clear and strong and wild. He could not place her accent, although her face and skin ruled out Caucasian. "I know," he murmured. "It's completely weird. I think we speak different languages. But somehow we can understand each other. Your words are not English when I first hear them. But it only lasts a split second. It was better the second time." He glanced around, suddenly suspicious, and half expecting a movie director to step out from the rocks and inform him that he was interrupting a scene.

Regardless, he decided she *was* crazy. Caution was necessary. He sniffed experimentally. "I can't smell her, either." He smothered a giggle. *Now* Shonika would have said something. "What a stupid thing to say," he blurted. "I mean, what did you say that for?"

The girl scowled but answered faster this time. "If I cannot smell her, then I do not know where she is. *You* at least I can see. And you certainly smell."

He brushed away pieces of barnacle still stuck in his forehead. His fingers came back more bloody than before. "No wonder I'm seeing and hearing things," he muttered. He showed her the blood. "I didn't mean to surprise you. And I wasn't spying. I was curious. If I'd known that you didn't want me here, I wouldn't have jumped down, and I'd have saved myself a smack on the head. What were you doing anyway?"

Her throwing arm relaxed.

"I was feeling the water. There has never been mist this early and it is warm."

Jonah stared at the swirling cloud. "Yeah, I noticed that, too. I don't know where it came from. It wasn't here a minute ago. But it saved my life on the cliff."

"Where are your people?"

He shrugged. "It's just me and my mom."

She lowered the rock. "The others are dead?"

"My dad's dead. How did you know about that?"

"I did not know. Where are the others?"

"The others . . . my family? Back in Vancouver, mostly." Their speech flowed easily now and he forgot for the moment that there had been a problem. He worried about the blood.

The girl looked at the outcrop from where he had fallen. "When did you make your crossing?"

"Crossing?" However pretty she was, her questions were crazy. His head hurt and he resented the comment about dead relatives. He needed water.

"When did you cross the ice?" She shook the rock impatiently and nodded toward the ocean.

"I don't know what you're talking about," he groaned. "My head feels like you just hit me with that rock."

"I did not hit you."

"I know. I was just saying it felt like . . . never mind. What ice?"

She fixed him with a stare that might have passed for sympathy, and he realized he must have looked an interesting sight with blood all over.

"It is there." She pointed.

Jonah squinted. "Why would there be ice on the ocean?"

She frowned. "There is always ice on the water."

"Weird," he muttered. "I feel weird. That *mist* is weird and *you* are weird."

The girl sensed the change in his voice and raised the rock. "If you run I will strike you."

"Why?" He held his aching head. "Why would you do that? Why can't you be normal?"

"If you run, you will tell the Crossers we are here. They will steal our food and we will die. Maybe you are one of them yourself."

"Listen," he moaned. "I told you. It's just me and my mother. No one else. And my mom isn't even photographing people. She won't care who you are." Tears sprang up again. He couldn't stop them. The pain was hot, pressing around his eyes. To make things worse, he was feeling nauseous. "I'm getting up now," he said weakly. "Then I am going to put my face in the water. If you want to crack my head open, I can't stop you."

"Wait," she commanded. "I need to tell the others."

"What others?"

"The others."

Exasperated, he waved his hands at the empty beach. "*What* others?"

The girl's scowl relaxed. "They are there."

"Where?"

She pointed. "You can see them, there. All of them walking around."

Completely crazy, he thought. He would have to show her to his mother. The girl needed help. A wild thought struck him: maybe she had fallen from the cliff, too!

"Can you not see them?" she asked.

"No!"

She lowered her rock. "You are bleeding above your eye," she said. "Perhaps it is why you cannot see them." She shifted her feet, moving closer. "Old Layban was struck by a bear years ago and lost his sight. The elders will know what to do." She brought the rock up close under his nose. "If you are being false with me, you should know that I can hit the middle of your head from thirty steps away."

"I know."

She stood, her hips shifting gracefully, each part of her body moving to a rhythm played by the sea. She waved.

At that moment his mother called.

The girl did not flinch.

Jonah waited. The girl should not be surprised to see her. At the same time, what would she do if he yelled? He cleared his throat.

"I'm here!" he called.

The girl swung around. She looked at the woods, then up to the cliffs.

"Hey." His mother's face appeared staring down at them from the outcrop.

"Mom." His cheeks flushed and he stood.

His mother did not look at the girl. "What are you doing?"

He pulled a face.

She saw the blood and sucked in a breath. "You're bleeding."

"I know."

The girl stepped toward him threateningly. "Who are you talking to?"

"My mom."

"Where is she?"

"Right there."

There was a long pause.

"Hey," his mother said softly. "Why are facing away from me? Look up here."

Jonah looked up. "What?"

"I'm up here. Who are you talking to?"

"To her."

"Who?"

The girl turned away quickly. She stood tall and dipped her head as if bowing to someone important. Then she pointed to Jonah and said to no one, "I found the boy here. He came from the sky."

Jonah peered at the beach beyond her. The girl was using a formal tone and had lost her hostility.

"The boy, standing there," she continued.

Again she listened. Jonah shook his head sadly.

His mother removed her cameras. "I'm coming down."

Without looking up he said, "No, Mom, don't. It's pretty far and you can't clear the ledge. I didn't."

His mother paced at the top searching for a way to get down. Jonah grimaced. He knew he must have sounded and looked terrible.

"You're bleeding pretty badly, Jonah. Are you hurt anywhere else?"

"Don't think so." Fascinated, he watched as the girl carried on.

"The boy just said, 'Do not come down.' I do not know what he means."

"She's crazy," Jonah remarked.

"Who's crazy?"

"The girl."

His mother paced faster. "I'm going to go back into the woods and get around this outcrop. I'll go quickly, all right? Don't move." She started, then came back. "And I'll get the medical kit."

"I need ice!" he groaned. His mother's face had gone white. "But I'll be okay. I'm just a little dizzy. And there's a lot going on here, in case you haven't noticed." And why hadn't she noticed? Not one question about his beach partner.

"I can't get you ice. But I have an instant freeze pack. Don't move."

"The boy wants ice," the girl told the air. "There is blood on his head."

"Better hurry, Mom," he said. "Crazy-girl is talking to thin air."

"Oh, Jonah," his mother stifled a gasp and disappeared from the cliff.

A gust of mist swept over them. When it cleared, he saw that the girl had dropped the rock and replaced it with a chunk of ice. The sun reflected as if she held an enormous jewel. She placed it in his waiting palms.

"They told me to clean your wound and rub the ice on it." Her hostility was gone. "The cut is as long as my small finger," she observed. "But not deep. The barnacles have made it jagged."

The ice was as cold as her fingers were warm, tracing the line of torn skin above his temple. He watched her neck as she worked, stretching, swallowing so close he could have touched her skin with his nose. There was a smell about her. Not a perfume or anything. It was organic. He wondered if she ever used deodorant. Another question to add to the list.

"You will hurt more from the bruise, I think," she murmured.

He liked her voice. His head bobbed against her touch, his eyes closed. He let the ice cool his racing thoughts.

Momentarily he asked, "Are there people standing near?"

"Yes."

"And you know them?"

"Yes."

"Do you know why I can't see them?"

"No."

"Can they see me?"

"No."

"But they can see you?"

"Yes."

Another tear squeezed out. "Could you see my mother when she was talking to me from the cliff?"

"No. I heard nothing and saw no one but you. There is no cliff."

He sniffed, wiped his nose with a sand-covered hand, then hugged his legs to his chest. "Well, it's not real. None of it is." He sighed. *It was a very clever unconsciousness.* He had suffered a concussion at least once before in his life and he knew that multiple concussions were dangerous.

"Your eyes are glazed like the ice," she noted. "Do you feel sick?"

"Mom will be here soon," Jonah muttered. "And then I'll wake up. But what am I going to say? 'Hi Mom! I'd like you to meet nobody and all her relatives.' I need to wake up. She's going to have a big freak and make me go home. She's going to think I'm crazy." He laid his head down. "Maybe I am crazy."

He felt his chin being lifted. He shivered but did not retract.

"Your skin is lighter than anyone's I have ever seen," the girl murmured. "If it were not for the sun's coloring, you would be white. And your hair is yellow. Where are you from? And why are you here alone?"

Jonah smiled. Neck . . . chin . . . lips . . . nose . . . eyes. Deep brown eyes. Such a beautiful dream. Except for smashing his head. Why did he have to imagine such extremes? The girl by herself would have been wonderful.

"Why would your mother think your thoughts are unsteady?"

"Because I am talking to nobody!"

"But I am here."

"Yes, and all your family, too. Mom will love that. She'll be quoting our grief counselor all night." A thought struck him. "What did your people say when you told them about me? Why are they just standing there? *If* they are there."

She dabbed at his cut. "The elders say that I am having a vision. We have been waiting for a new path since more Crossers were seen."

Jonah slapped his knees. "A vision. Perfect. I didn't expect that." He tilted his head to look at her from a different angle. "This must be a coma-state kind of thing, where my brain is pulling info from all over and jumbling it into some kind of nonsense."

She sat up. "Are you looking for a path, too?"

"I have heard," he carried on, "that people in a coma can have these life-like experiences. Out-of-body things. So if I am actually unconscious, then everything is only in my brain." He sighed. "You are the most beautiful unconsciousness I've ever had. You're so pretty that I don't really think you *could* be real."

She tried unsuccessfully to frown. "Your fear is less but you are talking foolishness."

"Foolishness?" He smiled. "Yes, you're right. I could even ask to kiss you and it wouldn't matter!" It was something he had dreamed of asking Shonika but never had the guts. Now, in the wilds, in the uncertainty of it all, somehow he felt safer. "Can I kiss you?"

She drew back and glanced uncertainly at the beach. Then she addressed the air again. "He wishes to kiss me."

Jonah smothered a laugh. Such a good coma!

The girl listened for a minute. "Will it help ease your pain? Or is it a custom?"

He stroked his chin thoughtfully. "It's a custom. And it would definitely help."

She repeated his words, then listened for a while longer.

Jonah glanced over his shoulder, wondering when his mother would come tromping up to destroy this magic. The girl was less confident now and he was enjoying the power shift.

"The elders are confused why you cannot see them. Even if the vision is for me alone, they do not know why your eyes are blinded to them. Because of this, the elders think that perhaps both of us are being shown something. They think it is best for us to watch and wait."

Jonah gaped. "I don't know how to respond to that."

"They also said," she added, "that I am permitted to kiss anyone I wish." When he raised his eyebrows she said, "*If* I wish it."

Silly, he thought. *No need to be nervous. My brain is making this up as I go.*

So.

Play on.

"And what do you wish?"

She regarded him steadily. "You cry a lot."

His dreamy grin fell. "I'd like to see what you'd do if a piece of your skull got stuck on a cliff." He waved his bloody hand.

She scowled. "And you waste words. Before my answer was broken, I meant to say that our men hardly ever cry after seven summers. I thought it was pleasant when you did."

"Oh."

"My father would not choose you, of course. Your arms are too thin and you would need to eat a whale to make it through a winter."

"I just asked for a kiss!" Jonah watched as she offered her palm, open and down, to him. He had seen her do it earlier when she spoke to the air and recognized it as a sign of trust.

"I am not trying to anger you. It is difficult to share my meaning when you break my words. Is this something your people do? And I am not a dream. I do not understand what is happening to you and me. You do not seem to know, either."

"No." The pain came in waves and he winced, waiting for it to pass. "No, I really don't."

They were silent for a moment. Then the girl said, "I have never seen anyone with blue eyes. And your hair is fair like the grass. Although you are strange, you are not unpleasant to look at. You are clever with your words, although they are too many." She nodded. "I like your crying, too, as long as it is not for every trouble."

"I don't cry all the time."

"I will kiss you."

"And I am not weak. I play hockey, you know, and I can take care of myself on the ice. What did you just say?"

"I will kiss you."

"You will?"

At that moment, his mother's running footfalls crunched along the beach. The girl did not appear to hear and remained as she was, her eyes tracing his lips.

"Hey, Jonah."

"Not now, Mom! Please."

The footsteps stopped. "What do you mean, 'Not now'?" his mother asked. Peripherally, he saw her kneeling and the red medical kit stark against the beach.

"My mother is here," he whispered.

"Of course I'm here, honey," his mother answered. "Your eyes are glazed," she noted. She felt his shoulder for broken bones.

He didn't resist and never took his eyes off the girl.

"I cannot see her," the girl said.

"I know."

His mother whispered, "Good. Now look at me. Look at me." She tried to move his head but he resisted.

She moved in front of him, only inches from the girl's chin, and squatted low to look into his eyes. His mother's forehead was creased with worry. Jonah looked over her shoulder and smiled at the girl.

"I need to check your level of consciousness, all right? I'm going to ask you some questions," his mother said. "They may seem silly, but I want you to answer. Let's begin. What is your name?" she asked slowly.

Jonah was quiet. Questions and confusion had followed him since the episode at the cliff top, and only seemed to be increasing. He needed time to think and sort his thoughts before he told his mother. If she knew even a fraction of what was happening inside his head, there would be swift consequences, including packing up and going home. There was adventure in the air and, other than the pain, it was better feeling a sense of excitement than of loss. Making up his mind, he reached around his mother, palm facing out. “My name is Jonah.”

Chapter Three

Jonah winced as his mother searched his cuts and his head. She ripped open a butterfly bandage. The girl was busy talking to the air again, and between her and his mother's questions, he simply wanted everyone to be quiet.

"This lump looked worse from the cliff," she said. "It's still ugly. How did your skin get so cold?"

He pointed to a patch of wet sand. "Ice."

Her frown deepened. "How are you doing?"

"Fine."

"What happened here, Jonah?"

"I fell," he said absently. "Bumped my head on the cliff. I'm fine now." He was distracted by the girl's agitated conversation with the air. His mother kept interrupting and he couldn't hear what was being said.

"So, who is this girl?"

He disengaged his stare. "That was a mistake."

"What do you mean? You said a girl was here. You even got mad at me."

"I was confused." He picked up a fistful of sand and let it sift through his fingers. "A dream or something." He saw his error as soon as the words were out of his mouth. He knew she would keep him talking, watching his eyes for dilation or slurred speech. She would assume a concussion.

"I don't like the sound of that. So you *were* unconscious?"

"No."

"Then it couldn't have been a dream," she suggested. Their eyes met but he quickly averted his. She was being more persistent than usual and he had to stay calm, buy himself time to think.

"Why don't you tell me what you saw?" she asked.

"Nothing to tell. I hit my head. I'm fine now. That's it."

"And the girl? Was she *nothing*, too?"

He nodded. "Nothing."

She ran her hands through her hair.

Jonah knew he wasn't acting predictably. It made his mother uneasy. It was as if her map was missing. He had to think clearly. But it was so hard. He just wanted to close his eyes for a few minutes.

She put the Band-Aid scraps into a resealable bag. "Jonah, look at me."

He turned to her. "What?"

"I think you should come with me to the float," she said.

"Why?"

"Let me rephrase that. You are coming to the float with me." The girl returned and knelt only a few feet from his mother.

"I have to go to the float," he repeated.

His mother turned to the beach. The emptiness seemed to make her shiver. "Yes, you have to go, and I'd like you to come now."

"I have to go now," he said to the girl, while at the same time trying to sound compliant for his mother's sake.

His mother stood and attached the pouch around her waist. "This place is freaking me out. I feel as if I'm interrupting a conversation." She swung around and, shielding her eyes from the sun, she found their footprints heading to the trees. "I have to tow your kayak. Try not to pitch over the side after mermaids."

The girl stood. "Where will you go?" she asked.

"To the float."

His mother grimaced. "What did you say?"

"Mom, I need to pee. Can you give me a second?"

She nodded. "You're not going to faint, are you?"

He waved her off. "No. I'm fine. I've got my wind back and I'm not dizzy anymore." He watched her walk up the beach. The girl's eyes were waiting. "We are leaving tomorrow morning. I can't remember the whole route." He paused. "To the hot springs. Then we go south, ending up at Ninstints, Anthony Island."

"We are going south as well." Her gaze flickered out to the sea. "A new village site has been found. I did not think anyone else knew about the hot springs. I also heard that we may leave the islands soon and return to the land that goes forever."

Everyone knows about the hot springs, Jonah thought. And what was the land that went on forever? The mainland?

"You mean, Vancouver? Alaska?" The names obviously meant nothing, so he tried again. "Back there? Way, way, east, where the islands touch the land again?"

"Yes."

"You came from there?"

"I do not know. It was before I was born."

The mist blew in, hiding the world from sight. "I don't know what to do," Jonah whispered.

She stared back, watchful, wild, and aware. "If you do not know," she answered, "then the way will be provided. Go where you must and go in peace."

His mother reached the top of the beach.

"I don't want to go. Something crazy is going on . . . ever since the mist appeared. I want to know what it is."

"Come on!" his mother called.

"I don't want to go," he leaned closer to the girl.

She tapped her chest. "What does your heart say?"

"I don't know."

"How can you not know what your heart says?"

"I don't know."

"Are you on a quest?" the girl persisted.

He pursed his lips. "I'm not sure. I guess I did ask for one. Sort of. I didn't really think it counted. It was more of a wish."

"Jonah, let's go!"

He glanced at his mother then back to the girl. "I don't understand anything right now," he started. "But this is what I am going to do. I'm going to go with Mom to the float. When we come back, I'll find you. My head will be clearer then. We will be back before sunset."

She nodded. "I will be here at sunset."

He nodded in return. Starting up the beach, he suddenly swung around. "Aren't you scared?"

"Why should I be afraid?"

"Because it's strange!"

"Jonah!" his mother called again.

"Coming!" He pointed to the sand. "Sunset, here."

"Sunset," she repeated. She showed him her open palm and he returned the sign.

Halfway to his mother he stopped again. They never kissed! He turned around. The girl was gone. It was possible she had edged around the outcrop but, with his mother waiting, he couldn't risk going back to look.

The float was a seven meter wooden island thirty meters offshore. Little space remained with kayaks stacked on the deck. His mother was calm again. She kept close watch on him, however.

"I need more black and white," she commanded. "There should

be twenty rolls in the box."

Jonah rummaged through the watertight bags. He spoke calmly, focusing on the task until he could reward himself with another look at the beach. Besides, his mother could not tolerate incompetence, and he had made enough mistakes for one day. "ASA 600 or 400?"

She snorted. "Four hundred. Look at the weather. And all my digital cameras, too, please." His mother was always fussing when packing gear.

"It could get cloudy, you know," Jonah said. "It changes quickly in the Charlottes."

"Four hundred," she repeated curtly. "And put four rolls in the Canon belt, two in the Nikon." As an afterthought she added, "Marine channel says we've got a high pressure system for five days. We'll be back by then."

He shook his head. "Why so much black and white?"

Another snort. "Anyone can shoot color."

She turned on her phone. Jonah heard "Bischofs" before the words were lost on the sea. For the past two hours he had wracked his brains, trying to answer ten thousand questions at once. Making his way to the float, he considered the possibility that nothing had occurred at all. The injury could account for a hallucination. But could his mind invent all the things the girl had said? And what had saved him on the cliff when he dropped the binoculars? That was not an ordinary gust of mist. He knew what his father would have said. It was a quote from Shakespeare's *Hamlet*. "There are more things in heaven and earth, Horatio, than are dreamt of in your philosophy." His father quoted it at every stunning seascape, mountain lookout, sunset—or when anything unusual happened.

He tugged at his lip. "And this is an unusual place," he murmured. He panned the bay with its tangled seaweed beds, the dangerous cliff tops and moody clouds. "You could find anything here," he reminded himself. "Absolutely anything." He thought again of the mist and the cliff top. "But can you trust what you find?"

He replayed the conversation in his head, cutting and pasting the girl's words in his mind. Taking a sip from his water bottle, he swirled it thoughtfully. It was something greater than a well-produced daydream. But why couldn't his mother see the girl? He shivered. A ghost? No. Her touch was real enough.

"How's your head?"

"Perfect," he said, without hesitating.

She gestured at a purple bag. "Toss that here." She stuffed wrapped tea bags into the bottom.

"Easy, Mom! That tea took a long time to pack."

"You should be drinking coffee," she teased.

"You've said that since I was four."

"It's true."

He pulled the bag away. "At least I won't die from caffeine cancer."

"Caffeine isn't carcinogenic."

"There are studies . . ."

"Okay, your head is definitely better." She looked at the gathering pile of photographic gear, her smile disappearing. "You scared me back there, Jonah."

He sealed the bag. "I know." He reached out and patted her knee. "Sorry, Mom."

"The cliff, then this . . . it's too much in one day," she said. "You're usually so good with your choices."

He nodded. "I'm being really careful now."

She sighed and pulled away. "I'm low in trust right now. And trouble usually comes in threes."

The afternoon sun warmed the side of his face as he settled

into his kayak. His mother pushed herself off from the float and her sunglasses reflected his brilliant PFD.

"If you drank coffee you'd be faster," she said and began to paddle.

"If you drank tea you'd be younger," he quipped.

With all the food and equipment, his kayak sat low in the water and he wiggled to test for tipping. *So wild out here,* he thought. The sun warmed but also scorched; the cool splash could freeze your blood in a wind.

Mist swirled about the trees. There was urgency in the air, an expectant wind that made Jonah feel alive and strong. His head no longer throbbed. The ice helped. He opened and closed his eyes quickly. No vision problems, no headaches, everything normal. He pushed his sunglasses in place and settled into the seat.

His mother waited for him. "I want you to stay with me once we tie up. I need your help."

"You've never *needed* my help. I'm just useful."

"Then I will need you to be useful when we get there."

In two hard strokes he passed her. "Careful is what you mean."

"Where does all the cheek come from?" she asked.

It was a delicate game. The girl would be waiting for him if he could convince his mother everything was normal.

From the moment he pulled off his spray skirt and stepped onto the beach, he shivered. *Be normal.* He took hold of the bow line and pulled the tough-shelled bottom over the barnacle-covered rocks. He stole a glance toward the far beach. Nothing.

"Not thinking of going back there, are you?" His mother stood ankle deep in the water. He took the tie rope and started to haul the second boat up the beach.

"Not right now. But I told you, there's an excellent fishing point at the headland and I still have to catch dinner."

She took the bow strap and helped him. With the camera gear in her kayak they never took chances with over-spray, not even with watertight bags. "Why don't we have that Mediterranean stew? Just boil some water and plop it in."

He grimaced. "Stuff tastes like dog food—I hate it. It gives me diarrhea."

"I like it."

They struggled with the gear-laden kayaks.

"These things are too heavy," he grunted.

"They fit the budget," she answered. "And not bad compared to the other options." His mother researched everything so thoroughly that the publisher she worked for had long stopped checking her receipts. They paid her well enough for a house, a car, even Jonah's future education. When his father died, the company had immediately increased his mother's salary. And the boats *were* quite good. In three days of beaching, they hardly showed a scratch.

Jonah collected driftwood for their fire, stacking it below the high tide line so the embers would be gone by morning. His mother pored over her maps, taking notes and occasionally making eye contact.

"I'm going for water," he said and lifted their small water pump.

Jonah moved slowly into the woods, past their tents and into denser bush. He felt cautious and the forest began to play with him, shadows and light slipping behind trunks. At the stream, he looked up from his work when a crackle of branches or shuffling boughs made him miss the mouth of the canteen. He was shaking by the time he broke into the sunlight, and the sheer relief of being out of the shadows made him sneeze.

"All right?" his mother called.

"Fine. Water is cold as ever." He placed the canteen within her reach. "I'm going to start moving the tents."

She looked up from her maps. "You still want to do that?"

"Yes."

She shrugged. "The sun will heat them up pretty badly if they're just sitting on the beach."

"The trees will cut off the light by the time everything's done. I'll be quick," he promised. The sun had started its western descent. He hurried back to the tents and began to empty two days of living from the orange domes onto a tarp. Refusing to look at the woods, Jonah moved his mother's sturdy three-man tent across the beach closer to the outcrop.

The biggest adventure of my life is waiting and I'm setting up a tent! By the time his own dome was finished, he was already planning the next step. He put his fishing rod beside a tackle box, then made his way to his mother.

"What are you reading?"

She didn't look up. "Physical evidence of the geographical formation of the islands. Are the tents ready?"

"Yes."

"Are they out of the sun?"

"Not yet." He looked up. "But they will be. Another half hour."

"I'd really like a nap."

"Take one!"

"What are you going to do?" She put the pages down.

"Fishing. Then I'll get dinner going."

She nodded. "No rock climbing?"

"No rock climbing. I'll walk around through the bush."

"Why do you have to go to the other side? There are fish right in front of us, you know."

"Mom, I'm a fisherman." Without pausing, he followed up quickly. "I know where they are . . . I smell them." In his mind he saw the girl sniffing the air for his mother.

She yawned. "I prefer you to stay within sight or calling distance."

"Why?"

"Come on, Jonah. I'm still a little nervous. This hasn't been your best day."

"Please, can I go? I promise you I'll be careful. I'll watch every step and I won't climb cliffs. I just want to fish! It's killing me, Mom! Look at all that water!" He waved at the ocean. "Millions of fish waiting for me." He pressed the argument a little further. "And you go away by yourself all the time into dangerous places. This isn't even dangerous. It's just fishing!"

She ruffled his hair. "Does it bother you when I go away? You've never mentioned it before."

He shrugged. "Sort of."

"Maybe I should take you more often. I just thought school was a stabilizer for you. You like it so much. And I love your friends. Shonika, Ben. They're good kids."

He nodded. They *were* good friends. But they had grown distant lately, not knowing how to act around someone who had lost a parent.

She touched the bump on his head. "Let's get through this trip before we plan the next. Don't wander far, okay?"

Jonah hurried to the tents, scooped up his rod and tackle box, and headed for the woods. He was back a few minutes later on the opposite side, standing in the waning sun. There was still no sign of the mist and he touched his temple, gently feeling the bump anew. He turned at the slightest sound or flicker of movement.

Shifting the rod to his opposite hand, Jonah waded in, watching his sandals find safe footing. He followed the rock cliff until he was up to his knees in water and could scramble onto a shelf. He was glad for his new footwear. The thick rubber soles came up at the sides and protected his toes, as well. The rock was covered with shells so sharp he could not sit. But Jonah had fished all his life, and standing on uneven ground was part of it.

The shells crunched beneath him and a million crustaceans gurgled voraciously.

"Hello," he said under his breath a few minutes later. He cast out, letting his line sink. "Hello!" he called a little louder. They had agreed to meet at sunset but he couldn't resist. He looked behind. "Hello, are you there?" Far to his left, his mother walked toward the tents. She carried nothing, a sure sign she was planning a nap.

"Anything?" she called.

"Nope."

"Try to catch something big. I'm hungry."

Her last words hardly reached him when his line lurched. His feet slid wildly as he tried to gain his footing, and black and blue shells scattered.

Ten minutes later, he tromped into camp with a two-pound Chinook hanging from his fingers.

"Darnedest thing," he muttered. His mother slept while he cut and cleaned the fish. His knife needed a good scrubbing before he reattached it to his shorts. He threw the guts into the sea where the waves would wash it far from camp. Nothing like having a bear rummage through their camp. It had happened before.

"Have to change that," he mumbled, looking down at his bloody shirt.

When he returned, his mother was awake and had lit two burners. Water boiled on one, while the other remained empty. A small fire crackled a short distance from the tents.

She wrinkled her nose. "The only second of the day I don't have a camera is the moment I lose the best shot. You look so cute, your messy hair, and fish dangling from your fingers."

"Waste of fuel," he nodded at the empty burner.

"I'm hungry," she answered. "And we have enough fuel to fly a jet around the world."

"It's not the same kind of fuel," he said.

She smirked. "Do you see why I usually travel alone?"

He pulled off his sticky shirt and removed his wading shoes. "I'm going to keep fishing after dinner, so you have to clean up."

"That's fair. You've done a lot today, Jonah."

They ate, staring at the calm water and the rising shadows of the trees to the east. He had so many questions. They came in waves, piling up for a time when he dared to share them.

"Delicious, Jonah!" She licked her fingers. "Incredible. You are so good at this. You would have made an excellent prehistoric survivor."

He started at her words.

"This is probably what they had for dinner most nights!" she continued.

"What do you know about the first people who came here?" While he couldn't explain why he felt the information was important, he knew the early travelers had been on his mind. And it was a relief from thinking about the mist.

"The big question."

He rolled his eyes. "What's that mean?"

"If you are a new, exciting, yet controversial theorist," she said, and swallowed her mouthful, "whom, I might add, I tend to like—then you believe that the first peoples may have used boats after crossing the Bering Strait. Probably about fourteen thousand years ago and, we think, much of the way down the coast by boat." She stared at the water. "This is what I'm writing about. It's why we're on this trip."

Frowning, Jonah asked, "Yes, but who were they?"

"Eurasians!"

He shrugged.

"Most of them came from Central Asia, possibly even Europe, then Alaska via the Bering Strait. It's called Beringia, the land bridge. The water was many feet lower than it is now. It was locked up by ice." She pointed to the water. "There would have been a flatland, a tundra, right there. Then they traveled down the coast until they ended here."

He swallowed hard and heard in his mind the voice of the girl describing the ice. He also recalled its cold touch on his temple. His next question came with great trepidation. "Was there a lot of ice in this area?"

"Tons. The ice froze enormous amounts of ocean, lowering the sea levels dramatically. They may have even been able to cross from the mainland to the Charlottes." She waved a finger to indicate where they were standing. "Parts that could not be walked on were navigated by boat. Just like we're doing."

"Crossed over," he repeated. "Crossers. What did they look like?"

She prodded her fork at him. "That's a good name. Crossers. I might use it for the article. More like migrants or travelers though, I think. I see them as early explorers, the first great discoverers. As for what they looked like . . . probably none of the groups were the same. From what I've read, they all came from different places across Europe and Asia, so they could have looked like a lot of people."

"Eurasians," he murmured. He pushed away an image of the girl in a dress and hurriedly asked, "What about the other theory?"

"Some archaeologists think the early travelers walked through an ice-free corridor of land, probably further east. Kind of like a geographic hallway all the way to South America."

He stared. "Why do you like the first theory?"

She shrugged. "Makes more sense. What would you do? Walk through dangerous wilderness, or float down the coast where you can fish or have fresh water every day?"

"I'd fish," Jonah said flatly.

His mother nodded. "The problem is that the coastal theory is hard to prove. Most of the coast where ancient people would have camped is now under water. Remember I said the ice locked up the water? It's difficult to find evidence that's been submerged for so long. But there would have been grass, even trees, bears, goats . . . imagine that."

"Imagine that," he repeated.

"And you would have made a good Crosser, Jonah. A good cook, anyway."

The fading sun reminded him that some of the answers he was looking for could be on the beach at sunset. "Practice," he answered absently. "My mother never cooks."

"Yes, but she cleans."

He stood up. "And I'll leave you to it."

She looked mildly amused at his plate. "The cook doesn't eat his own cooking?"

"Not tonight. There's fishing to do." He felt her eyes on his back as he walked toward the cliff.

"Jonah?"

He turned.

"You forgot your tackle box."

"Uh . . . I don't need it. I'm just going to cast." The sand was cool and Jonah regretted not wearing his sandals. He had also forgotten a shirt. He glanced at his wiry, tanned body. What had the girl said? That he would eat a whole whale through the winter. What did that mean? Wasn't it healthy to eat a lot?

A trail of smoke drifted above the water. On a second look, he saw a haze forming against the far trees. Not a campfire. It was bigger. His heart beat against his chest, drumming anticipation and fear. He entered the woods.

"Don't run, don't run," he cautioned and thrust the branches aside.

Even in the dim of the darkening woods, he could see that the mist had returned. When he stepped onto the opposite beach, he froze. His fishing pole clattered to the stones. He scooped it up without taking his eyes off the figure a hundred steps away.

She hadn't seen him yet. Her black hair hung wildly down her back and her slender arms covered her chest, her fingertips touching her mouth.

Jonah ran. She turned, smiling.

He had not meant to get so close but found that she also had stepped toward him. Brown eyes searched his, patient, waiting, seeking.

The mist swirled, whipping around their bodies, tugging, even pulling.

"Hi," he waved his hands foolishly.

The girl raised her palms mimicking his gesture. "Good meeting," she answered.

Jonah slapped his hands against hers with a loud smack.

When their palms touched, a rush of sound, a thousand echoes, vibrated through their fingers. The colors of the sky, earth, and sea blended into a rain behind the girl's astonished face. She looked upward. *Otherness* overwhelmed them.

A voice, a deep, powerful rumble, uttered a single command.

"Come."

Jonah staggered back.

The sunset returned, the sky painted as before. The mist was gone. Falling onto his backside, he was open-mouthed. His arms tingled and the sensation spread down his legs. "What happened?" he gasped. He sat up straight.

"Who are you?" The girl sank to her knees.

"Who are *you*?" he retorted.

"I am Akilah."

Jonah clenched his fists. "But *who* are you . . . *what* are you? What just happened?"

Akilah recoiled further. "I was hoping you would know. As for my name, you know it, for I have told you. I am one of the People." Her voice was loaded with disappointment.

Jonah squeezed his eyes shut.

"I've got to tell Mom. I've got . . ."

She looked up. "I heard the voice, too."

He scanned the heavens, and with a trembling voice he asked, "Do you know where it came from?"

She nodded. "I think, yes."

"Well, who or what is it?"

"Why do you not know?"

"Because I don't."

"Can you not *feel* who it is?"

"No," he grumbled. Then he shifted uncomfortably. "Well, I might! But even if I did, why would I trust anyone who takes away someone's father?" The words popped out before he realized their meaning. He added quickly, fear rising in his chest, "I'm going." He could not look at her. He could think only of getting back to camp.

Akilah made a grab for his wrist. "Wait!"

"Don't touch me!" he screamed.

"I'm afraid, as well," she said. "There is fear in my heart. I have never heard the voice before."

"Just tell me what's happening!"

"I do not know! The elders told me to be calm of heart, but you make it difficult."

"Why are you on this beach?" he demanded.

"Why are *you* on this beach?" she flung back. "Every day we live in fear—sickness, Crossers, hunger, cold. And you turn back. Go! Run to your mother. Run away, you, Jonah-boy. I will listen."

He took a tentative step. "Don't you see that this is unnatural? That *you* are unnatural?" His face reddened.

She glared. "That is not what you called me earlier."

The smell of campfire smoke reached them. He breathed the comforting familiar scent.

"Sorry. I can't explain anything and it's making me feel strange."

"I feel the strangeness, as well."

"But you're part of it! I found you wading . . ."

"You found *me*?" Akilah pointed. "You jumped from the sky and scared me so badly I almost threw a rock at your head."

He snorted. "Yeah, but look at you. You're wearing a bearskin, your hair is all wild, and you talk funny. It's like you're a cave girl or something."

She touched her hair and played with a strand. "Your hair is yellow like the sun. That is enough to make the children laugh. No one has yellow hair. And you speak words quickly as if they have no purpose."

Silence.

"I can't explain this," he finally huffed.

"Why do you need to explain it? Why must you know the answers before traveling the path?" she asked.

He clenched his fists. "Because I'm confused . . . and scared."

She nodded. "The elders say that I have been chosen to take the path and find the good for us in it. But I can not go on this quest if you run away. It is only when we are together that anything seems to happen."

"A quest?" He thought for a moment. "Can we trust this . . . voice?"

"I do," she said solemnly. "I felt nothing untrustworthy."

"You *felt*! That's not exactly reassuring. I don't have a lot of trust right now. That was the most unnatural thing ever. I need time! I know there's an explanation. There always is. The problem is that usually there's a bunch of people figuring it out. I've only got Mom. And I can't tell her. My dad, at least, would have listened. But he's gone."

Akilah shuffled her feet angrily. "The voice has spoken for as long as the People have memory. You make it seem as if there are no messages for the people of your time."

"What?" he asked.

"Must you make your decisions with so much thinking?"

He threw up his hands. "*Does* this happen to you every day?"

"Never before. Can you not feel that this is a quest? There is no one around. We are being sent on a journey. The answers are not given at the beginning. It is at the end that they are found. First we must listen and seek."

Jonah kicked at the sand. "I don't have to do anything except find my way home."

They fell into an awkward silence, staring, watching. Jonah focused on her eyes. Not a flicker of deceit, not a hint of secrecy. While he agonized, a breeze brushed his face and he felt the bracing confidence of the sea. Despite his frustration, he sucked in a deep breath of cool, strong, ocean air.

Far out from shore and nestled against the cliffs, the mist made a wide circle around them. It pulsated in enormous rhythms, like a dog pulling on a leash, waiting for the command to attack. A deafening rumble of thunder filled the air. Jonah watched it gather with growing concern.

"Oh no," he murmured. "I think it's coming back."

The mist returned with the fury of a tempest. It came from all sides, gusting from the trees and off the water. Then it began to thicken in wide bands, so quickly he hardly grasped what was happening. The coils of mist concentrated around Akilah. The clouds were dense and both of them were instantly soaked. The beach hissed as the wind tore through pebbles and shells.

"Jonah!" Akilah screamed. The mist swirled tighter around the girl's legs, rising and thickening. "Jonah!" she gasped.

Jonah jumped into the heart of the mist and reached for Akilah.

Chapter Four

Wind, water, air, and sky blended together in a tumult and Jonah lost all sense of their surroundings. A tingling sensation vibrated through his body.

"Do not let go." Akilah's teeth were clenched as tightly as her eyes.

The *otherness* had returned, surrounding them like wind. Jonah drew her head to his chest and she wrapped her arms around him. They shivered.

And then it stopped.

They were standing on stone with the sky streaking red. The ocean sounded far more distant than it should. It was cold. Very cold. And there was a buzzing sound. He shivered and a cloud of flies swarmed off, only to return a second later. A wind gusted and swept the bugs away.

"Nothing happened," Akilah whispered.

Jonah released her. "Yes, it did." The ground extended out almost a hundred meters beyond where it should have. Instead of sand, there was tundra stretched out like an uncut crop in a farmer's field. He searched farther, cupping his hands to the sides of his head. The ocean was still there but it didn't come close to shore until the next headland. There, the water crashed in frothy waves, pasting the shore with the kind of punches only seen in a west coast winter. He stared at his feet, wanting to see puddles and low-tide pools. Instead, the ankle-high grass filled the gaps where the water had been. It didn't look like an island anymore. He reached for his map. Then his eyes locked on another change, closer, and even more worrisome.

Three hundred meters away, a large white object moved on the water, making its way to the open ocean. "Ice," he murmured.

Here and there, large chunks lay on the ground like dying snowballs in the waning sun.

Akilah completed a full circle, a frown growing on her face. "The People are gone."

Jonah looked for his mother's campfire, but where the outcrop should have been, a flat plain stretched past the headland to the horizon. He could have been standing on the edge of a prairie. There were no tents, no kayaks, and no other people. His skin goose-bumped and he wished that he had not released Akilah.

"It's not real, though," he whispered. "I mean, it can't actually be there." He took a swipe at the ice so far away. In the distance he could see tall mountains with white tops, and further to the east a white mass that seemed to go on forever.

"Glacier," he droned.

Akilah paled. "Where are the People?"

"Where is my mother?" he whispered. "Where are we?" Panic rose in his throat. "Give me your hands!"

He squeezed her hands. Nothing happened. He changed his grip and shook her shoulders. "Come on!" he shouted to the sky. "Bring us back! Do you have to take everything away from me? Even my mother!"

Ripping free, Akilah pushed him away. "Do not do that!" she shouted.

"I want to go back," he gasped. "We've got to go back. Akilah, please. We've got to try."

She backed up further. "Go where?"

"To the beach," he gasped. "Where we started."

"This is where we started. Except that the People are gone."

He waved. "Maybe this is where *you* started. Not me. Now, come here." He reached for her again. She backed up and took a wide stance. She flared her eyes and hissed.

"Oh, don't be stupid," Jonah growled. Jumping forward, he caught her arms. The wrestle escalated quickly to a fight. Akilah struck him twice before he could get a good grip. Stunned, he tried to push her away and found that she was already pulling him right past her and onto the ground. Before he could recover, she was sitting on his stomach and pinning his arms above his head.

"You little idiot," he hissed. He struggled for a moment and then began to thump her back with his knees.

"Jonah! Nothing is happening," she gasped. "Our hands are touching and nothing is happening."

He stopped.

Her hair fell onto his face and once again their skin was close enough to touch, the tips of their noses inches away. He blew a lock of her hair from his eyes. The stone against his back, though fiercely cold, was reassuringly solid. He felt a bead of sweat trickle down the side of his temple. The anger had been refreshing and cleared his mind.

"Get off," he grunted.

"No. You are wild. It is safer for me to sit on you."

He brought his knees up letting them touch the small of her back. "I could knock you off if I wanted to," he told her. "I'm calm now, Akilah. I am."

She tightened her grip.

"You're right," he said softly. "We are touching and nothing has happened. I get it. Sometimes I need to go a little crazy before I calm down. Let me look around and think."

She watched his eyes and sniffed uncertainly. Then she rolled off and sat up. "I do not know where the People have gone."

Jonah hugged his chest. "It's so cold. I should have changed my shirt."

"I put my furs down over there," she said. "While waiting for you. They may still be there. And this wind will not last long. It never does. It will be warm again soon."

He followed her onto the rock shelf toward the water. Sure enough, only a short distance away they found a small pile of her belongings. Jonah stared at the thick skin she handed him. It was crudely yet cleverly stitched. He pulled it on. It reached to his waist. There was fur on the inside all down the chest and back.

Akilah smirked.

"I feel like a monkey," he muttered.

She touched his side. "It is worn the other way. The fur should be on the outside."

"Ah. Of course."

Akilah threw another skin over her shoulder and picked up a small pouch. She touched the rock on which her clothes had lain. "The People had to leave quickly." Worry filled her face.

Jonah knelt. On the stone were several marks.

"They were in danger." Akilah raised her head and sniffed. "Crossers, likely." She held the pouch up for Jonah to see. "It is good they left this behind."

"What is it?" he asked.

She opened the leather bag to reveal several objects. Two appeared to be knives, made of stone. Another was a bone needle. The last looked like a piece of string.

"What are they?"

"Needle, thread, spark stone, knife. None of the People walk without them." She smiled. "There will be strong words for me for leaving these." Her face darkened again. "It was not my fault! I did not go far. The mist covered me."

Jonah tapped her shoulder. "Hey. If you're right and we are on a quest . . . then you've got the best excuse in the world."

She nodded gratefully. "I will need to look at the grasses to see which way they went, and what made them leave."

Jonah's teeth chattered incessantly, and from the pounding of his heart he knew it was not from the cold alone. "I can't think straight," he said.

Akilah slid the extra skin over her head. Despite his anxiety, Jonah could see that she had given him the warmer skin.

"You had better shed it quickly."

"Shed what?"

"Your fear. I need you to think clearly. And the animals can sense it."

"Whatever," he muttered. He blew on his hands. "You said, 'Crossers,' right?"

She nodded.

"Crossers." When he rubbed his face, the rough leather at his wrists scraped his chin. He looked out at the ice, the grassy plain, the steeply falling landscape, and the ocean so much farther away than it should have been. "This is what Mom said it would be like thousands of years ago," he whispered. "At least fourteen thousand."

Akilah eyed him warily. "Are you going to be wild again?"

The vast tundra swirled around him. He held his balance. "No. I'm just figuring things out." He gave her a long stare.

"Are you warm?"

He nodded. "Yes, thank you."

"I will look at the grass now," she said. "The People may not be far." She scanned the sky. "It will be dark soon. We will need to decide our path."

Jonah suddenly felt strangely calm. He could not tell if terror had sent him into shock or if the cold had numbed his brain. More than anything, it was a sense of helplessness that allowed him to move. "Okay." In the back of his mind was the niggling reminder that he was suddenly experiencing the very thing he had asked for: a quest. But why did it have to be so difficult? The wind nudged him. "I'm going, I'm going," he murmured.

He followed her across the grass to higher ground. The grass stems stood almost to his knees and rippled like a barley field in the wind.

"Where are we?"

There was a trail of broken grass ahead and Akilah made for it. "Stay on the path," she warned him. "I must see what has happened." She stopped where several converging paths turned east toward the sea. Grass was trampled everywhere. The remains of several circles with new criss-crossing paths were barely distinguishable.

"Crossers," Akilah stared.

"How do you know?"

"I have witnessed this before. See the old fire at the center? It has been smeared, stamped in anger and rage."

"There is nothing left," Jonah whispered. "Nothing. Not even a scrap of garbage. If it wasn't for the trampled grass, it would look as if no one had been here."

"Everything is taken," Akilah declared. "Everything is used many times. And even if something was dropped, the Crossers would have taken it."

"Do you think anybody was hurt?"

Akilah stepped into the clearing, stooping and touching the bent grass. "They left quickly but with order," she said with relief. "There was time. The People escaped," she began. "No blood. There was probably enough warning. Crossers do not like to fight. A surprise kill is best. They want food, skins, sometimes a male or female to replace another lost in their own tribe. But it looks as if they were seen in time."

Watching her, bent low as she was and combing the grasses, he suddenly thought out loud: "You're a Crosser, too!"

She turned sharply and glared as if he had sworn at her. "We are not Crossers."

"But you must have been," he countered. "You came from the mainland, too. I'm sorry. I didn't mean anything by it."

"It was a long time ago," she said. "Beyond my memory." She straightened and held her head up proudly. "We are the People."

And the Crossers are immigrants, Jonah thought. Some things never changed.

She lifted a chip of charcoal. "How can this be?"

Jonah took it from her. "What's wrong?"

"This coal is at least a day old. When I met you, just before sunset, the fire was still burning." She looked at him nervously. "The time *has* changed."

He grunted. "Nothing surprises me anymore. Can you tell where they went?"

"Yes. We always make several paths, to fool our attackers. But our escape has always been by the sea. We are skillful with boats," she added. "More so than others we have met. It has always been our way. It is how we came from the north." She pointed to a path leading down to the seashore. "That is the path they would take." She faced the opposite direction. Several careening paths sloped downward from a distant hill where a patch of green stood out from the grasses. "The Crossers came from there."

Jonah imagined fur-clad cavemen charging down the hill. He squinted. There was something there. "Are those trees?" he pointed to the hill.

"Yes. We try to camp where there is wood. We use moss from the grasses for fire, but the wood is used for many other things. It is harder to find."

Jonah ripped a stem from the ground and twirled it. "What now?" He felt uneasy with the light beginning to fade.

"There are some caves near the sea that will be safe. We keep our boats there. Most of the Crossers do not like to be near the water at night."

"Why?"

"They fear the water and only use boats when they have to."

"I like boats," Jonah said. He took comfort from the idea. It was good to be better at something than an opponent. It was always an advantage in hockey. But this was not a game. The Crossers aimed to kill.

In the growing dusk, Jonah followed the girl's swiftly moving figure, flapping his arms to keep warm. He knew how to walk with a resigned step. He had followed his mother a hundred times. Akilah was in constant motion, looking back, sniffing, or leaning down to snatch things from the ground.

"What is that?" he asked when she ripped a handful of orange flowers and stuck them in her pouch.

"Dinner," she answered.

Jonah reached for his map. The sound of the crinkling paper made Akilah stop.

"It's weird," he muttered. He angled the paper, searching for better light. "We've been walking south-easterly. There should not be a rock shelf here. It's as if the water has gone way out . . ." He slapped his head. "Is there a lot more ice somewhere? Out there?" He indicated eastward.

She pointed southward. "Over there. Across the water. Lots of it."

"Unbelievable," he murmured. "It's unbelievable. This *is* thousands of years ago. The ice has locked up the water and lowered the sea level. I'm walking below the level of the ocean. Do you get it? This is prehistory." He wondered at her. "You're ancient. You came down the coast in boats. Your people, you're the first ones. You and the Crossers."

Akilah tensed her shoulders and crouched, ready to spring. "You are being strange again," she cautioned.

"Please," he whispered. "What is going on?" He went down on one knee. "Why am I here? Where is here? When is here?" His breath came in gasps and he felt his heart pounding.

Akilah stood over him. "Get up."

Jonah gripped his throat, not even hearing her.

"Get up," Akilah said again and tugged on his shoulders. He dropped to all fours, like a dog, trying to find his breath. He was going to pass out. He hated passing out.

She hit him. Her palm caught him on the side of the head and he fell over. "Jonah, stand up! We have to get to the caves before nightfall. Do you understand?"

She raised her arm again. As she swung down he caught her wrist and aimed a punch with his free fist. He managed to stop an inch from her face. "Do that again," he panted, "and I'll break your nose." His vision cleared and his breathing eased. He lowered his arm.

She smiled. "That is better."

"Thank you," he whispered.

"We have to go."

"I know. I'll follow."

Chapter Five

The cave was hidden at the tip of the headland, out of sight of the higher plains and close to the water. The dwindling light revealed a cavernous mouth more than two meters high and a meter wide. Akilah sniffed. "No one has been here for some time."

"It's pretty dark," Jonah whispered. He touched the damp rock. "Will the tide reach here?"

"No. We can start a fire," Akilah suggested. "The wind comes from the sea and the caves are deep. The smoke will keep inside. We should look for wood—there may be bits closer to the water. It will be cold tonight; the ice winds are blowing."

They worked their way down to the water. Although there were chunks of ice startlingly close, the sea itself was familiar. "At least it's not purple," he mumbled. He shivered and fought another wave of panic. He started whistling.

"Do not make that sound," Akilah scolded. "The noise will travel far."

Kicking the pebbles, Jonah muttered, "What is everyone's problem with whistling?"

Just beyond the tide line they found some sticks.

"The beach has been gleaned," Akilah explained. "But there is always something new." She was right. Jonah found three crooked branches thicker than his arm, caught beneath a jutting slab of stone.

Akilah's eyes sparkled. "Look what you have found!"

He shrugged. "I'm used to finding a lot more than this. Obviously, things are a little different here. I could have found this much in ten seconds back . . . back in my time."

She gave him a thoughtful stare. "I would like to see a place . . . in the years ahead, as you say . . . that has so many trees."

They returned to the cave, Akilah carrying a jumble of moss, seaweed, a chunk of ice, and Jonah hauling the wood.

The tunnel twisted within a few meters of the entrance and the wind stilled. Jonah shivered. "I can't see anything. What if there *is* someone in there?"

Akilah leaned into the darkness. "I have smelled. There is nothing. Not even an animal."

"Wait!" he nudged her aside and put his burden down. He pulled out his knife. At the end of it was a small penlight with a new battery. He flicked out the largest blade as a precaution. When the light clicked on, Akilah started and gave a shriek.

"There is light coming from your fingers!"

Jonah snorted. "No! It's a flashlight. On the end of my knife."

She unraveled his hand and peered closely. "How have you captured the light?"

The beam shot across to the opposite wall and she shrieked again in pure delight.

"This is a wonderful thing."

He let her take it. She rolled the beam wildly all over the cave walls and ceiling.

"Okay, okay," Jonah grabbed it. "You're making me dizzy. Point it at our feet. So we know where we are going."

"I like the flashlightning."

"Flashlight."

"Flashlight," she repeated. "This is very clever of the people in the years ahead."

The cave opened into a larger cavern. "Look!" Akilah cried. The beam settled on a bundle of sticks and what looked like an animal.

Jonah stiffened. "What is it?"

"They have left more wood. And a boat."

Jonah approached cautiously and lifted a floppy skin that stretched even as it left the ground. "This is a boat?"

"Yes." The flashlight beam bobbed.

Curved pieces of bone lay underneath it. "This is the frame?"

"Yes."

"Wow. Can't wait to see what this thing can do."

Akilah placed the light down on a stone so it shone between them. He could just make out her face.

"Start the fire," she ordered. "I will make the boat."

Bewildered, he reached into his pockets searching for matches. Unsuccessful, he picked up two sticks propped against the wall beside the boat. The top two pieces were bigger than the rest. A large, flat piece of bone was attached to each end. He motioned with them helplessly.

"If you burn those," Akilah said impatiently, "we cannot paddle the boat tomorrow."

He grunted. "I can't start a fire. No matches."

"I do not know about matches," she answered. "The sparking stone is in my pouch. And there is dry moss and twigs from the branches. It is more than we usually have to make flames."

He glared at her shadowy figure. "I can try. I've never made a fire without matches. I've tried but it's really hard. Mom never has—no, she did. In Africa," he growled. "Where is that sparking stone?"

A long while later, he had not generated even a puff of smoke. Akilah knelt to examine his progress. His fingers were cut, and he had broken the sparking stone. He sat dejectedly over the small pile of moss and sticks.

"Why did you stop?" she touched the base of the sticks.

"I can't do it," he groaned. "There's too much wind. The sparks are too small. I need a flame."

The girl examined his work. "You are close. The sparks have darkened the moss here and here," she pointed. "Give me the stone. You gave up too easily."

In the beam of his penlight, he watched her take the splintered rock. Her small hands turned them over expertly. "You forgot to make a windscreen."

He winced. Stupid. Stupid. How many fires had he made in the wilds? Inexcusable. He lay down with his back to the entrance in order to block the wind.

Akilah shook her head. "No. Build one. Eventually, you will want to get up. The windscreen must stay."

Jonah looked about the cave. "The boat?"

She shrugged.

He took the circular frame, admiring the perfectly stretched skin and its surprising weightlessness. Two whale ribs, highly polished, criss-crossed along the bottom and gave the craft its depth of less than a meter. Jonah placed the boat across the width of the cave. The wind tugged and sent it crashing to the floor. He tried again.

"It keeps falling."

"Use something else."

"There is nothing else!" he said angrily. He could hear her striking the stone repeatedly.

"You must find something." She spoke as if addressing a child.

Furious, Jonah felt about the floor, still supporting the structure with one hand. It twisted away.

"Stupid, stupid, stupid thing!" he yelled. His voice echoed.

"Be quiet!" Akilah commanded. "Are you so weak in your thinking as to call the Crossers?"

Pushing the boat away from where Akilah was attempting to start the fire, he pulled the warm animal skin from his back. Crumpling the fur into a bundle he knelt down beside the girl. "There!" he growled. He placed the bundle behind the pile of moss, raising it as high as he could to block the cold air. "Good enough for you?"

Akilah focused on the moss. "You want everything so quickly. My father taught me patience. He made me stand in the rain once when I became frustrated over my first fire. Warmth is important; more so than anger. But I was four summers old then."

And then the sparks began to jump. Little rock fireflies were leaping the gap from her hands to the sticks. She was making the tiny sparks land on the moss.

"How did you capture the light in your hands?" Jonah murmured.

She smiled.

He shivered.

"It is close," Akilah whispered as a tiny plume of smoke rose from the pile. She blew gently, so gently, and a tiny glow appeared at the base.

"Please," Jonah whispered. "Please."

A flame flickered into life.

"Sticks," Akilah reached.

Jonah scrambled for the pile of twigs.

"*Now* lie down behind it. We cannot risk it scattering."

The cold air blew over his back and he concentrated on the flames. The wood caught.

A small crackle echoed around them and Jonah gave a shout

of triumph. A wave of heat reached his chest. He flipped over. The sensation was bizarre. His back had been cold for so long that the heat rippled over his skin like liquid, neither hot nor cold. *Heat and cold*, he thought. *Always extremes out here. Just like her.*

When he turned, she was placing shells close to the fire.

"What are you doing?"

"Making food."

His mouth watered. As their little blaze brought more light into the cave, he saw that she was preparing other items as well. With her knife she clipped bits of grass, lichen, and even a small length of seaweed, each placed purposefully in front of her knees. The shells closest to the fire were beginning to open. They were bivalves, steaming clams.

He touched a glistening shell. "These ones are good. I've made them before, too, with my dad on a fishing trip."

"We can eat now," Akilah said. She scraped a clam from its shell, slid it onto a bed of lichen and grass, then wrapped it in seaweed. She offered it to him.

He crinkled his nose. "Is it safe?"

She pulled back.

"No offence," Jonah said. Sniffing, he tried again. "How do you know it's okay to eat?"

She said nothing.

"Akilah. Sorry. I've never seen this stuff before. I mean, the grassy stuff. The red flowers. I've eaten seaweed before and clams. We could get sick, you know."

She scowled and looked up from the fire. "It is sweet grass. Usually I boil it for a count of twenty before adding the lichen and shells. Then I give it some sea salt. The broth must boil four counts of twenty. More sweet grass is added and then long-stem green leaf. We have nothing to cook it in. So, I must make it this way."

"Oh." He looked at the little bundles sitting at her feet, ready for eating. "How do you know all that?"

She took a piece of seaweed and examined it. "I must."

He watched her fold the rubbery flap, reinserting one end into a tiny slit she had made with her knife. The contents of the bundle fit inside perfectly, gift-wrapped from the sea.

"What do you mean?"

"Everyone must know what to eat."

"What does that mean?"

Akilah put the food down. She took the leather pouch from her side and opened it for him to see. There were many kinds of shells, dried grasses, and plants of various colors. "I remember what is good to eat, so that I do not die from eating the wrong food. Even the smallest children must learn the berries, roots, fish, and shells."

Jonah blew out a long breath. The severity of her words reminded him of his mother getting angry at him at the cliff edge. "You can't make mistakes here." He took the food. The seaweed was rubbery and, other than the strong taste of brine, he could have been eating sushi. "Excellent," he chomped. "Exquisite. Pure perfection."

She stared.

"I like it," he finished. "You know, the crazy thing is that all Mom has to do is take pictures. We get a bunch of money and then we buy all our groceries. You have to work for it." He ate three more bundles, then remembered her comment about the whale. "How old are you?"

She folded another piece of seaweed. "I am twelve winters old, almost twelve. Old enough to be a *watcher*."

"What's that?"

"It is what I was doing when we met. I watch for danger, for Crossers."

Jonah shifted uncomfortably. "Have you seen them . . . the Crossers, coming . . . before?"

"Yes. Two times. I have good eyesight."

"So do I! My mom sometimes calls me Hawkeye." They exchanged smiles.

Jonah felt the last bite of food reach his stomach. "Good."

Akilah placed a small chunk of ice inside a shell. It melted near the fire and she offered it to him as a drink. Their fingertips touched.

"I figured you were about my age," Jonah sniffed at the shell.

"What do *you* do for your people?" Akilah queried.

He swallowed the warm water. "Lots of things. Not like you, though. It's a lot more serious here." He struggled for words. "I fish . . . and I collect firewood," he began.

"So you are a hunter?"

"Yeah. I'm a hunter."

"Have you killed a bear?"

"No."

She averted her eyes. "Good."

"Why?"

"Do you want some more water?"

He shook his head. "Why are you anxious about bears? Is there one around here?"

"What happens when you kill a bear?" she asked.

Not an easy answer. They had almost hit a bear in the car on the way to the Charlottes. But people did hunt for food. Didn't they? "Well, sometimes you end up with a lot of meat. And other times you end up in jail. It depends on the season and where you live."

She turned her head sideways and looked at him through the corners of her eyes. She had done this before and he realized that it had meaning. The last time she had made the gesture she was holding a rock. "Do they honor you for the hunt?"

"It's different. Some people get pretty angry about killing animals. What do they do *here*?"

She looked away.

"What do they do here?" he repeated.

"It is a boy's passing into manhood to kill a bear with the other men."

"Oh."

She wrapped more seaweed.

"Well, I have not killed a bear," he said. "And I haven't hunted anything except fish and bugs." He swiped at the air, pretending to catch a fly. Aiming an imaginary spear, he thrust it at the *bug* in his fist.

Akilah laughed and slapped his knee.

Jonah flared his eyes and hissed, imitating Akilah's posturing. She slapped his knee again, a little harder.

The remaining food was carefully placed back in Akilah's pouch. She kept the largest shell, then told Jonah to go and put the others at the entrance.

He looked into the gloom. "Now?"

"Yes. It is time to sleep. Be quick, Jonah. It is easier to become cold than warm."

"Why am I putting them at the entrance?"

"If anyone tries to come in, they will step on the shells and we will hear them."

"You said no one comes here at night," he accused.

"Those were not my words. I said the Crossers do not like the water. Take your wrap—the fire is strong enough on its own now."

He waved her comment aside. "I don't need it." The warmth of the fire had worked into his muscles and he meant to show her he was tough. He stumbled forward. The low ceiling forced him to duck and the blast of cold that rushed around his body was a chilly reminder of the absence of modern comforts.

It was not the blackness he was expecting. Instead, the entrance glimmered with a frosty light, glossy and wet.

The moon reflected boldly across the sea. Its brilliance shimmered in the nearby pools. He looked up and gasped. Twenty thousand stars sang over him, some in clusters so full they were in danger of spilling out of their heavenly places. Shooting stars blazed at the corners of his vision so quickly that he could not keep up with their fiery tails.

The sound of a rock turning pulled his attention back to earth. He could smell grass and ocean, earth and seaweed, an untamed abundance. The fields they had come from that afternoon were a vast gray shadow.

"What in the cosmos is going on?" he whispered. He ran his hand through his salt-coarsened hair. "I'm wide awake in a dream." He squatted, balancing on the balls of his feet. "Don't worry, Mom. I'm okay."

He must have looked a strange, shadowy figure from below, leaning on his haunches as he was and staring out from the cave. "I'm a caveman," he snorted. Suddenly, he lowered his voice as far as it could go and grunted. Then he swung his arms from side to side. "Woman in cave," he grunted. He burst into giggles. His smile disappeared. *I'm going crazy.*

It was not long before the chill worked into his bones. But his desire to show Akilah his strength made him stay. Hopping from one foot to another he counted to a hundred, feeling every bite of the night air. "Good thing Mom's not seeing this," he mumbled between chattering teeth. *You're not using your head!* That's what she'd say. "Maybe, Mom, maybe. But if you saw this girl . . . if you could see what I see right now."

He counted again.

Before returning, he spread the small collection of shells just inside the shadow of the opening. His fingers were shaking.

Akilah sat close to the fire. The firelight accentuated her high cheekbones and the eyes that had so often bewildered him that day. There was nothing about her that seemed cave-like anymore. She was skilled beyond comprehension, trained to survive in this world of extremes. She could build a fire from nothing, make food from the sea, and knew how to construct a boat from animal skins. And now she was right: he was cold.

He sat opposite her. "Why am I here?" The words came out sloppily.

She looked up. "You are freezing."

"I'm useless. I couldn't build a fire. I couldn't even find a good windscreen. I don't know how to do anything that you do. Nothing. I'm an idiot out here. What is the point?" He sounded drunk.

"Sit closer to the fire, Jonah. I told you not to be so long. You must not be careless with cold."

He shrugged. "I'm not a hunter. I'm not much good without my tackle box, and I'm completely helpless without a gun when it comes to bears." He slapped his hand against the stone, coming dangerously close to the edge of the flames.

Akilah started up, alarmed. "We should sleep now," she said quietly. "Please, Jonah. Be calm now." She motioned for him to lie down. She spread a wrap on the floor close to the fire.

Clumsily, Jonah made it to his knees without falling over, then lurched onto his side with a crash. "Sorry," he muttered.

They slept under the boat. His wasted time near the cave entrance had drained all his warmth away. He lay on his side, his back to Akilah, and brought his knees up to his chest, hugging them in fetal position. The chill seeped through the skin covering the stone floor. He could hardly feel his legs below his shorts.

"We should get in the boat," Akilah said. "The floor is too cold."

Flipping the boat, they placed it as close to the fire as they dared, then climbed in.

The sides were high enough to block the coldest breezes. The boat skin was thicker than their clothes and held back the cold from the floor.

"We should share wraps," she said a moment later. Without the flashlight, only a little firelight flickered on the low ceiling.

He felt her tugging. Like a little child he sat up, allowed her to strip it off him, then lay down again, shivering. She placed it over both of them and he sensed her spreading the wraps across his numb legs.

"Turn and face the fire," she commanded. His legs wouldn't move. *What a stupid way to die . . .*

Akilah snuggled behind him. She wrapped an arm around his waist and pulled him close into the curve of the boat's walls. "The fire will warm the sides, at least for a while. There is not enough wood to keep it alight all night."

"Do you ever get used to this?" Jonah chattered.

"The People spend many nights in the cold. But I have Elik and my mother to keep me warm, especially when the snows come. In bad weather, we sleep two families together."

A short while later, Jonah felt some warmth in his back and shoulders where Akilah touched him. He became aware of other senses. Akilah's hair smelled briny and for the briefest moment he thought he smelled urine. The sudden worry that he had wet himself made him shift his position.

"Do not move," she commanded. "It raises the coverings and the heat escapes."

"Sorry," Jonah murmured again. He shivered. No, he had not peed. It was her. She smelled. Not only faint traces of urine but of body odor as well. He wrinkled his nose. Perhaps he didn't smell so pleasant himself. Soon the warmth of their bodies began to spread and he flexed his fingers. The pain of returning circulation made his eyes water.

"Hurts!" he grumbled.

"Yes." She was still awake.

He found her hand and closed his own around it.

CHAPTER SIX

THE CRASH OF BREAKING SURF BROUGHT JONAH OUT OF A DEEP SLEEP. His whole side ached and his face tingled. He could not feel Akilah behind him anymore. It was lighter in the cave above the rim of the boat. He sat up. The air was smoky and the fire still burned. A new pile of sticks was piled against the wall. Akilah was gone.

Jonah stood drunkenly and stretched to the roof, then flapped his arms in the chill. His breath flowed in wispy clouds and he knelt to retrieve his wrap. Stepping out of the boat, he reached for the welcoming flames, going as close as he dared. He took out his penknife and shone it into the edges of the cave. Empty.

A gust scattered ash over his knees and brought the embers into full life. He grabbed the boat and set it upside down so that its width blocked the wind.

"Why didn't I do that last night?" he said out loud. And why hadn't Akilah thought of it either? Maybe she had and just wanted him to figure it out himself. Or maybe she had been too busy lighting the fire. He stared at the waning fire. She had saved him last night.

He left the warmth of the flames and tucked the wrap tightly around his chest. A moment later he shaded his eyes and stood rocking back and forth on his heels. *Oh, Mother! If you could see this!*

Enormous chunks of ice floated on the sea like a fleet of white ships, their chilly sails cutting the sky with icy sheets. He caught a cold blast of their passing. The sky was so blue! Three birds, black and white cormorants, flew overhead. The birds checked their flight and turned back to the beach, landing only meters from a lone figure.

The instant he saw her, he was flooded with an overwhelming sense of loyalty, a fierce appreciation deep as blood. Jonah walked, taking in the sky and the giant ice floes behind her. The beauty of the morning made her all the more amazing. The cool air was intoxicating. He wanted to hug her—to kiss her.

As he neared the water's edge, she opened her hands and showed him her finds of the morning. Seven or eight black shells gleamed up at him. They were much larger than the ones of the night before.

"You look warmer," she said. "And your hair is so bright in the sun. I can hardly look at you."

He nodded. "Thank you for taking care of me last night. I was being stupid. I shouldn't have . . ." He kissed her.

It was the fastest he had moved since they arrived, and her surprise made him laugh. Her lips were cold but soft.

Jonah bent over quickly to pick up a rock. He threw wildly and the stone clattered noisily before bouncing into the shallows.

"That is a nice greeting," Akilah said. "Is it a morning greeting?"

"Not for just anyone," he grinned. He flapped his arms like a bird and ran on the tundra in wide circles around Akilah. She tried turning to keep up with him but soon staggered with dizziness. When his circles shortened, she grabbed his out-flung arm, then abruptly they released each other.

Akilah poked at the shells. "I found them over there."

He had seen many kinds of shells before. These ones looked like some he had seen in Australia with his mother.

"They're nice."

"We need to leave soon. They may come back this way."

Jonah scanned the land beyond the cave. He knew she meant Crossers. The tundra was empty, and yet everywhere he sensed movement. The air was full of birds. The rippling grasses held scurrying creatures whose heads popped up to stare at them. On the highlands he could see animals grazing. Even the wet ground crackled with living things making their way to and from the sea.

"*Teeming*," he murmured.

Akilah looked at him.

"It's teeming with life," he said. "Everything is moving. It doesn't look like this . . . where Mom is." He pointed to the herd against the low hill. "What are those?"

"Goats."

"Goats?"

She tapped the wrap he was wearing. "Goats. And you are wearing it the wrong way again."

He felt the crackling skin and rubbed his thumb on the coarse hair inside. "It's almost like fur."

Akilah looked past him to the highlands. "It is not like this, where you are from?"

"No. Well, sort of. We have a lot more trees. We don't have so many creatures. Or, if we do, they hide more. The ocean is the same. Except for the ice."

Akilah put the shells in her pouch. "There are more animals at night."

"Dangerous?"

She re-tied her pouch. "Everything is dangerous. Come. We need to get the boat from the cave and leave."

Even the food here could kill you if you did not know what to eat. He thought of the freezing night they had just spent and hurried after her.

"Can I have a few minutes?" he called. "I want to do something. For you." She flinched when he reached for her pouch. He took out the thickest thread and one of her needles. "Wait here," he commanded. "I may be a while." He felt her watching him as he slipped behind two large stones. When he returned less than ten minutes later, a fish dangled from a line.

"You *are* a fisherman!" she laughed, and shook her head in amazement. Jonah basked in the compliment.

They ate in the cave, using the last of the coals to cook the fish. Akilah scattered the fire and made two false trails away from the cave. Then they took the boat apart and made their way to the sea.

Jonah watched her out of the corner of his eye. She was so lean. Her arms were strong and wiry and her hands never stopped moving, gleaning the world around them.

Akilah stooped a moment later to pick up several yellow flowers growing outside the tide line.

"More breakfast?" he asked.

"No." She tucked one behind her ear. "Pretty."

They reassembled the boat just out of reach of the surging tide.

"We should head south," Akilah said. "The People are heading south."

"How far?"

"I do not know. A new camp was found."

Jonah reached for his map. "Can you remember anything else?"

She straightened. "I remember one thing that was exciting. A place was found that has hot water pools to swim in! It is said to be sacred."

"Hot water pools?" Jonah rubbed his chin. "Hot Spring Island." He traced the lines while she watched. "There. Hot Spring. But it's east, not south."

Akilah looked uncertain.

"Can you remember anything else?"

She nodded. "I remember one of our people had seen the place where the world ended. The land came to an end and there was nothing but ocean going on forever. I do not know if we were going there. These were the words being told to the elders, and I heard them with my own ears."

Jonah swatted at a cloud of bugs. "The last of the Charlottes is Khungit Island, or Anthony Island. See?" He pointed to the end of South Moresby Park. "Mom and I were going there at the end of the trip before getting picked up in Raspberry Cove." He squinted. "There is a village there. At least, there is in my time. We could head that way. Perhaps we will find your people along the way."

She regarded him intently. "How do you know where all the places are?"

He shrugged. "It's a map. It shows where everything is. Where I am from, we know every little bay and river." He frowned. "I keep saying *where* but *when* is more accurate." He shook his head. It was not good to think about it. *Focus, Jonah, focus.*

Akilah traced one of the islands with her finger. "We have something like this. It is a memory of our journey. But there are many more pictures. Does this tell your story?"

Jonah flipped the map over to examine the back. "I don't think so. It's just a map."

The ice floes continued to sail past, white, intermittent shapes on an otherwise blue horizon. Cold air made Jonah shiver.

"It'll be freezing out there," he commented.

Akilah dragged the boat through the remaining grass and on to the stony shore. "It can be very hot, too. But we will get away from the ice soon."

"That's encouraging." There was so much he did not know and the list was steadily growing. "So, south, or east?"

Akilah splashed into the shallows. "I think south."

"South it is." Jonah noted her bare feet as she waded without complaint amid a myriad of barnacles. He dumped the wood into the skin belly of the boat, then threw the extra skin on top.

"Wrap it," Akilah said sharply.

Reaching down, he put the sticks in the middle of the skin and folded it over. "Good enough?"

"Yes."

"You're worse than my mother."

"If the wood gets wet . . ."

"I know, I know. We'll freeze. Like I said, you're worse than Mom."

The thought struck him that his parents would have done something like this before he was born—traveling together in remote places in their kayaks. His mother handled the details—food, equipment, maps. His father enjoyed the unpredictability of adventure and always requested more spontaneity. Now Jonah was far from both parents, on his own adventure and traveling with a single companion. He blushed at the thought of Akilah as his wife.

The water was freezing and he jumped into the middle of the skin belly before they cleared the shallows.

"It's freezing!"

"Get out."

"It's freezing!" he repeated.

"Get out."

They swayed unsteadily in the first of a succession of swells. He stepped back into the shallows, cursing. They waded until he could no longer feel his feet. His eyes, however, took in everything. At his ankles, silver, orange, and purple creatures gleamed and moved in their own micro world. It was just like the tide pools back at De la Beche. Except more of everything.

"Now get in," Akilah commanded. "Sit toward one side and spread your hands out along the skin to keep it steady."

With his feet so numb, he piled in awkwardly this time. But he put his hands out as she asked and held the circular frame firmly while she got in. The bottom bubbled and Jonah feared they would be sucked down. Then the middle rose up again and jiggled like a waterbed floating on the sea. The frame held fast.

He laughed. "This is good." Akilah reached for a paddle. "Do you know how to use this?"

He nodded and examined the rustic tool. It was as cleverly constructed as the boat and made from a stout piece of peeled branch. It had a wide flat bone inserted at the end. Thin leather straps wound multiple times through small holes in the wood, and bone bound the shaft and blade together.

"Shoulder blade," he noted, holding it up. "What kind of creature?"

"Bear."

"Did you make this?" he asked.

"No."

"Father? Brother?"

"No. An elder made it."

Jonah dipped his paddle. The blade bent with the pressure but still managed to pull well against the water. It wasn't what he was used to. A little floppy. "Do you have brothers and sisters?"

"Yes. Twelve."

"Twelve!"

A wave lifted them and he raised his paddle to ride it. He turned to see her staring judiciously. "I can paddle!" he said defensively.

"I've kayaked since I was seven. Watch!"

Akilah studied his confident strokes with satisfaction. "I was worried you could not keep up with me. Still, your timing is not correct. We are going in circles. We must paddle together, strength for strength. There is a rhythm to it. You must feel it."

She was right. It was not like any boat he had ever paddled. For one thing, it was round. Every stroke had an instant effect and sent the boat into a spin if it was not counterbalanced. And it was so odd to sit *beside* someone in such a small boat. It reminded him of rowing a dory but without the benefit of oarlocks.

"Good!" she encouraged. "Now look ahead to the near headland. We must both aim for the same place. Find the rhythm. There! Can you feel it?"

For the next few minutes, Jonah concentrated on his strokes. His shoulders soon began to tire.

"So," he puffed. "Your mom's had twelve kids?" He couldn't imagine his own mother having any more than one.

"I am the only child of my mother and the youngest of all my brothers and sisters," Akilah broke his concentration. "Elik has three mates."

Jonah couldn't restrain a gasp. "I don't know anyone with three wives. It's illegal where I come from."

"What does that mean?"

He had to shout as they approached the headland. The waves crashed uproariously. "You can only have one mate at a time! Some people only have one for their whole lives."

"And your father?"

He knew it was coming. The question always came at some point. "When he was alive he had only my mother."

She didn't say anything for a while. He stole a glance at her face, but she was turned away, watching her paddle. Then she said,

"Now it is up to you."

"What is up to me?"

"To honor your father. You are part of him. So he lives on inside of you. It is a great honor. I will live my best for Elik and my mother when the time comes."

No one had ever said anything like that before. For a moment, Jonah forgot his tired muscles. "He died rock climbing, not long ago."

"Elik likes to rock climb. He tries to find nests for the People. My mother says that he will fall one day."

"No, no," Jonah shook his head. "My father was climbing for fun. It was his sport."

"Yes," Akilah agreed. "Elik likes to climb for fun, too. I do not think that he is really trying to find eggs most of the time. I think he likes to be up high and see the land and sky and feel like an ant for a while."

"Mom hasn't forgiven him."

There was a long silence. Then Akilah turned. "Is your mother's thinking unsteady?"

He shrugged. "Why do you say that?"

"How could your father climb another cliff, or hunt, or swim, or anything else? One day Elik will make a mistake. His foot will slip or his bow will break because he did not tend it. My mother and I will not hold this against him. He is Elik. My father. Has he not always loved us? It is Elik who stays awake to watch us when the storms come. It is Elik who is last to eat when the hunt returns with little."

"I never thought of that," Jonah murmured. "Maybe that's why my mom is so upset. She's not so mad. She's sad. Because he loved us. In a thousand little ways."

"Yes!" Akilah affirmed.

Jonah continued to think aloud. “Once, she said that Dad acted with his heart, not his head. She thinks I’m careless, too, and that I’ll get killed. Can’t blame her. Sometimes I do things without thinking. Like at the cliff. I think she wishes I was a little more like her.”

“It is good to think with your heart, too. It makes you proud and strong. It is how we know the Maker,” Akilah said. She gave Jonah a knowing stare. “You are here with me because you made a heart decision.”

“That’s true.”

Then she added, “I am sure your father is proud of you for coming with me.”

Jonah felt a lump in his throat. “Maybe, yeah. I’d like that. A lot. My mom tries so hard. She spends all her time with me when she’s not on trips. We’re close. But we miss him so much.” He thought for a moment. “I like talking about my dad. I don’t do it enough.” He added softly, “Dad would have loved this. He always told me that the things we believe in with our hearts are as real as what we can see with our eyes. I’ve always struggled with that idea. Not now.”

There was a moment of silence between them; then Akilah said, “You must have a small camp, if you can only have one mate.”

Jonah laughed. “No, no. There are a lot of us.”

“How many?”

He raised his paddle to the sky and the blade flashed in the sun. “More than the stars.”

Akilah snorted.

“It’s true!” he protested. “Mom says we can see about twenty thousand stars on a clear night with the naked eye. That’s the size of a very small town.”

“More than the stars,” Akilah repeated. “That is too many. How can you breathe?”

“Yeah, you’re getting the idea.”

Akilah was quiet for a few minutes, and then she asked, "Are there people that look like me where you come from?"

She was certainly more beautiful than anyone he could think of, Jonah thought. But he knew it was not what she meant. "Yes, many. Many nations."

"Many nations," she repeated. Her eyes glistened. "Good."

The wind eased and the chop was not as intense near the shore. He was happy, too; they were going south. Anything was better than being near the ice.

They approached the tip of a headland when Akilah stiffened. The shore was no more than eight meters away, closer than she had ever let them get since the start. She sat up and stopped paddling. The crows were being wild in the trees high above.

The cliff face beside them rose to a towering height, glimmering with rainbow-colored water droplets. A gurgling waterfall tumbled down the rock face soothingly.

"I am not feeling safe," Akilah announced.

"What's wrong?"

She indicated upwards. "The birds will not rest. They are circling and unsettled."

"So?"

"It means there is something else up there."

The words had hardly left her mouth when a stone the size of Jonah's head struck the water only a meter or two away. A splash of cold ocean caught him in the face.

"Paddle!" Akilah yelled.

Jonah stared at the cliff top, half dazed.

"Paddle!" Akilah screamed. "They are throwing rocks!"

More rocks landed like bombs and filled the air with spray.

"Idiots!" he yelled. "Are they trying to hit us?"

"Yes," Akilah said grimly. "And they are trying to kill us."

Chapter Seven

Akilah paddled furiously. The water churned as jagged rocks pounded into the sea. Their boat floundered. They both instinctively tried to steer, sending the boat into circles.

"Let me do it!" Jonah gasped.

"No! Paddle together. Stare ahead!"

Jonah leaned forward and concentrated. More rocks landed, one of them striking the edge of their boat. The lip buckled and dipped dangerously close to the surface.

Jonah's breath whistled in his throat. He was paddling so hard the shaft bent like a bow. The girl groaned beside him. Out of the corner of his eye, Jonah saw a large stone tumble from her back. It rolled, striking his side. Akilah swayed dizzily.

"Akilah!"

Her head drooped, her paddle idle at her knees. The bottom of the boat sagged downward with the weight of the stone and he was thrown off balance. Jonah tried to keep paddling, but the boat only turned in a slow circle.

He shook her. "Akilah!"

She lifted her head drunkenly. Another stone landed beside them. Their eyes met.

"Get down!" Jonah gasped. "Let me paddle." She leaned forward weakly and he began to stroke, first one side and then the other. Every second he expected a stone to crash onto his head.

He worked harder, and slowly, painfully, they pulled away from the cliff. The rocks began to fall short. Akilah gulped for air and whimpered frequently.

Jonah looked back. Several figures stood against the skyline. Fierce-looking men peered down. There were at least a dozen, no longer hiding but watching. One or two of them carried spears. They were the most terrifying sight he had ever seen.

Suddenly, obscenities poured out of his mouth. A rage boiled inside and he screamed at the figures through tears. One of them shifted against the blue sky, but they said nothing.

He set his paddle on the curve of the frame and wiped the sweat from his eyes. The stone had ragged edges and had torn through his shorts at the hip. He managed to heft the rock over the side. Akilah was silent and unmoving.

He sucked in a deep breath. "Akilah! Akilah?"

She stirred.

"Oh, thank God," he half sobbed. He touched her shoulder. "You're not bleeding. At least, I can't see anything." He moved her hair off her shoulder. The stone had left a wet mark but had not torn her garment. Goat skin was tough.

She was still wheezing.

He gently touched the back of her head. "You okay?" he asked. "We should get you to shore so you can lie down."

She grimaced. "We cannot land here. They will follow. Along the coast."

"What do they want with us?" Jonah fought to keep his voice in control.

With an effort she answered, "The boat is useful to them. Our clothes, too."

Jonah shivered. An image flashed through his head of the pair of them lying on the cold ground, dead, with a spearman ripping the clothes from their bodies.

"Never, never!" he cried. "They will *not* get us!" Strength from his new resolve flowed through his arms and cleared his mind. "The Bischofs, then." He indicated to the east. "It's the way to Hot Spring Island as well."

The distance looked vast.

Akilah winced. "It may be that the People have gone there. I do not know for sure. It could be that they ran from these Crossers as we are doing." She took a deep breath, then added, "Elik would have fought them if they were a small band, or if they met them on land when the boats had been pulled ashore. I am worried about my mother. Is there no safe place?"

Jonah's hands shook. "Can you paddle?"

"For a while. I will need to rest . . . often."

"Fine with me. I'm so scared right now I could paddle across the ocean." He had meant to say, *angry*, but recognized the other emotion fueling his blood.

Clouds were building to the east and a shadow grew across the surface of the sea. "It doesn't look that far. I can see the land. It is much farther . . . where I come from."

"You are a good paddler, Jonah," Akilah said a moment later. "If I had been alone . . ."

"But you weren't," he interrupted. "Just like I wasn't alone last night."

She sighed and looked enviously at the clouds. "I'm thirsty."

The pain in her eyes made him desperate. "Let's paddle and get you something to drink at the first safe place. Don't worry! I'll get you water if I have to squeeze it out of a Crosser's beard!"

The next hour was grueling. Akilah stopped frequently. There was a dark stain on her shoulder, a patch that should have dried long ago. Jonah winced. She might need stitches. Or maybe it was broken. He would have to look at it. Yet the air was rich with oxygen and, with the Crossers far behind them, Jonah took courage. The sun, when it broke through the cloud, was warm and the world around him was full of color.

"Rest?" he puffed, after a while. Jonah squared his shoulders, massaging his sore neck. His palms were raw with blisters. He looked around. They were in the middle of a large body of water. The clouds had grown thick and dark, racing along beside them in their mirrored reflection. He pulled out the map.

"That's the Bischofs," he pointed ahead. "At least, where they are supposed to be. Can you pull us straight?" He waited while she adjusted her strokes. The map flapped wildly. "Hot Spring is a little south and we've been going the right way. I hope the wind stays with us." Akilah did not look as pale and her responses were quicker. They might just make it.

Over his shoulder he could still see where the attack had occurred. "Why is everything so violent here?" he wondered aloud. "Why do they have to kill us to get our stuff?"

Akilah reached into her pouch and pulled out a root. "Can you cut this? It hurts when I grip." He leaned over to help."Would you have given them the boat?" she asked. "Would you let them have our clothes?"

Jonah shook his head. "No. I would fight. But why not just take it? I mean, we're kids." He bit into the root and sucked out the moisture. There was hardly any taste but it took away the dryness. The boat caught a swell and Jonah felt a significant rise and fall. The wind was getting stronger.

Akilah chewed thoughtfully. "It is better to kill from a distance, from a height, or with a spear. There is less danger. When you get close, it is easier to be killed or hurt."

Jonah nodded. "I get that. Soldiers used to fight really close. I guess that's why they invented arrows . . . or guns. Still," he brushed his hair from his eyes, "there are other ways of getting things without killing." He glanced up to see Akilah shaking her head. "You don't think so?" he asked.

"No. It is too hard without my skins, my knife, or my pouch. I would kill to keep them. Especially in winter. "

He shifted uncomfortably at her words. Jonah had enjoyed hundreds of conversations at school about what he would do in certain situations. He always liked the topic. Now he faced the real thing. "Have you ever . . . ?"

"No. Elik has always been there for me." She gave a little groan and touched her arm.

"Lean over," he urged. "Let me look."

The armhole of her clothes was fairly wide, but it was still wet and stuck closely to her skin. He took a breath. Gingerly, he peeled back the edge of the tunic and peeked inside.

"It's very raw," he announced. "And it looks like it might go blue. I can't see too well."

She smothered a groan. "Pour some water on it."

"You sure?"

"Yes."

Jonah scooped some sea water with his hands and poured it over her shoulder. She grimaced.

"You're the one who needs ice now." Then he added, "Or maybe the hot springs! I know you're supposed to put ice on wounds, but the hot water can ease soreness, too. This is going to be tough."

Within half an hour Akilah was reduced to steering. Jonah fought his bone paddle.

"Let the blade bend, then stroke," Akilah told him.

"It's still not very good," he grumbled. Their pace increased, however, as Jonah relaxed and the rocky shoreline grew clearer.

"Wait a second." Jonah stared closely. He pulled out his map. "There are too many islands. That can't be the Bischofs."

"Is your picture-map wrong?"

"No. There are just too many islands. What does that mean?" He stared at the rising land. "Why so many?" he whispered. "Think, think, think." The Bischofs were still islands, at least, and not an unrecognizable land mass.

"Water levels," he mumbled. "Mom said the water levels were lower. I've already seen that. So there are more islands because the water is lower and exposes them. Maybe not even islands. Just more of the Bischofs." He folded the map. "Imagine that! I'm seeing parts of the Bischofs nobody from my time has seen before!"

Akilah frowned uncertainly.

"We're good!" Jonah said triumphantly. "At least, I think we are."

Something bumped beneath the boat. Akilah raised her paddle like a spear in readiness. "What is it? Can you see?"

The body of a seal, bloated and missing half its tail, rolled over in their wake, its sightless eyes staring back grotesquely.

"Turn back!" Akilah shouted.

He shrugged. "It's dead."

"I know!" she said impatiently.

"Akilah, the sky is getting black. We need to get to the Bischofs. I don't want to be caught in bad weather out here."

"We need that seal skin," she replied briskly. "More than bathing in hot springs. It is not common to be given a seal without great effort."

The bobbing seal was huge. Jonah had grown up seeing seals on the west coast but not this big. "Anything for you!" he sang.

"Pull it in," Akilah indicated with her paddle. They leaned forward and sculled the seal to the edge. Jonah shuddered when his blade touched the heavy body. The pelt was gray and mottled near the head. A gaping wound in its tail showed where a larger mammal had made its attack. Jonah regarded the dark water uneasily.

"Now what?"

Akilah reached to her waist and began to loosen the thin leather tie. "We tow her."

"It's a girl?"

"Yes. Quite old. Not so fast a swimmer any more. She almost got away."

Jonah looked at the shimmering body. "It's a shame."

"She is a gift to us." Akilah pointed to the bundle of wrapped sticks behind him. "We need a branch. It needs to be thick, like this, and almost as long as my arm."

Puzzled, Jonah did as he was told. Akilah took her knife and began to sharpen one end of the wood to a fierce point. She tied one end of the leather belt to the stick and the other she laid under her knee. Then she sat down on top of it.

Kneeling, she leaned toward the seal.

"Hold my waist," she said to him.

"Huh?"

"Put your hands on my waist, so I do not fall out."

He placed his hands on either side of her hips.

She faced him and their noses touched. "I do not think that is strong enough."

"No problem." He wrapped his arms around her.

"Do not move," she warned.

"Wouldn't dream of it."

"Jonah."

"Sorry. I've got you."

Akilah made herself as tall as she could and aimed the sharpened stick at the seal.

"Oh no!" Jonah groaned. "Not a good idea." He felt her plunging downward and their boat bubbled. The stick bounced as if it had hit rubber and suddenly the girl was in his lap. The boat rolled horribly and buckled. Then the skin popped back up.

"Let go of me," Akilah said. "Let me go. It did not work."

When he sat up, Akilah re-sharpened the broken stick. Her injured shoulder was obviously causing her pain. "Do not pull on me so hard," she said. "You must stop me from going too far forward if the spear slides on the seal."

"Okay," he said. "But I think it's stupid to try and get a dead seal when your arm is hurt and we're in the middle of the ocean."

She looked up angrily. "It is a *whole* seal. How can you say I should not do this? You cannot stay alive for one night and yet you are telling me I should not have this seal."

"Why did you bring that up?" he shot back. When she did not reply, he said, "Fourteen thousand years and we're still arguing the same way. Where I come from, when you do something stupid like I did last night, and you say, 'Sorry,' then it's over. It's forgiven. You don't keep bringing it up as if I just did it again." He put the paddle across his knees. "That's what Shonika does to me all the time. She brings up stuff I did weeks ago. I hate that."

Akilah gazed at the land in the distance. She took a deep breath. Then she tilted her head to one side and ran her hand affectionately along the seal's skin. "Elik says that when we forgive someone, we must not even remember the offence. It is forgotten. Just as the beach forgets the waves of yesterday." She looked at Jonah. "I will leave the seal."

He stared at the dead creature. It bobbed with the swells as he patted its thick side. "If I ever get back alive, Shonika is in for some surprises."

Akilah frowned. "Is she your intended mate?"

Jonah burst out laughing. "Shonika? Never! Give me the stupid spear!"

They eased the boat to Jonah's side. He hefted the stake experimentally. Akilah tugged on his throwing arm. "All is well with you?"

"I can do this," he replied. He licked his lips. "Imagine it's a fish," he whispered. "It's just a fish." Akilah's bear hug was reassuring. At least if they fell in, they would go together. "Ready?"

"Yes."

He raised the spear. There was a horrible squelching sound as the stake burst the skin and a shuddering jar rippled all the way to his shoulders.

When he opened his eyes there was dark ooze on his fingers and splatter on his arms. He gagged.

"Good! Good!" Akilah chirped. She reached around him and tested the stake wiggling it back and forth.

"Don't!" Jonah gasped. "Or I'll throw up." The spear stood upright near the head, and the seal bobbed on the water like a narwhal. "Please, God, let there be nothing larger than a seal near us," Jonah murmured. "We're towing a meal for a whale."

The rain began to fall as they tugged the boat onto the shore. The sandy soil and fresh-smelling grass filled them with hope. Birds swooped and skimmed the tops of the grasses. A duck landed in a nearby pool.

"That's a Common Muir," Jonah muttered as they reeled in the seal. "Didn't know they lived back then . . . now."

They took a drink from a stream cutting its way through the tundra to the sea. Akilah was struggling.

"How is your shoulder?"

"I am sore."

He put his hand gently on her back as she stooped. "Let's get out of the rain. Is it safe here on the grass?"

Akilah stood stiffly. She sniffed and looked in each direction. "We are safe from Crossers while the rain lasts. No one travels in the rain. It can be dangerous to get wet unless it is necessary."

He lifted the boat to bring it higher up on the grass when she stopped him. "The seal should be skinned soon. Bears do not worry about rain."

"What should I do?"

She held out her knife. "Can you skin it?"

He shook his head. "I don't know how. It's a little different from a fish. Can you?"

"I need to rest. And it is hard to pull the skin off."

"Okay, let's rest. Then we . . . pull the skin."

They found a depression in the tundra and dragged the boat and seal through the soaking grass. The hollow was deep enough to use the boat as a shield while still allowing a view out the sides. Akilah wanted to put the seal between them but Jonah refused.

"I'm not sitting beside a dead seal. I don't care if a bear comes." He stared at the carcass.

With a snort, Akilah lay down. Just before she closed her eyes, she sniffed the air and took one last look around. "Do not fall asleep, Jonah."

"Me? I'm fourteen thousand years old. Why should I sleep?"

"Do not sleep."

He sat uncomfortably against the grassy bank and watched her settle. The rain drummed steadily on their shelter. Somewhere nearby the ducks quacked in their rain-filled pond.

Jonah stole a peek at the seal. It looked like it was sleeping, too. "Don't invite any of your mammal friends, okay?" he whispered.

Chapter Eight

The afternoon light was all wrong when Jonah glanced out from their shelter. Something had disturbed his long nap. He listened. No rain. No ducks. He let his eyes close again.

Somewhere nearby came a low, rumbling snuffle. He seized the edge of the boat. The seal was still there. He found Akilah's hand and squeezed.

She jerked awake. She put her fingers on his lips before he said anything. Reaching for her knife, she sniffed and listened. She pointed to the skin covering that held their supply of wood. She made a fist. He nodded and noiselessly removed a big stick.

Jonah hefted the stick. She motioned for him to re-tie the bundle. When he turned back, she was gone. Cursing, he scrambled out. He found her crouched and peering over the embankment. Fifteen meters away, the most terrifying mammal of the Charlottes raised its head. The bear's fur bristled with deep browns and hints of gold. The size of its rippling shoulders made it clear that Jonah's paddle blade must have come from a cub.

The bear leaned forward and flared its black muzzle. The ice-winds were blowing and, for once, Jonah appreciated the glaciers on the ancient mainland. For with his warmth, they also stole his scent. They only had a short time to act; the bear would eventually sense them. It sat down on its haunches and raised a paw to scratch its nose. Then it rolled onto one side with a powerful sigh. It kicked its legs playfully before flipping to its back for a scratch against the earth. *In another time, this could be a circus bear*, Jonah thought. There was a wild beauty to the creature. He felt like he was invading someone's privacy. After all, it was the bear's land. No question about that.

Akilah motioned. She pointed to the seal, then at him. Finally, she nodded toward the water, twenty meters away. He shook his head. No! The bear would see them. Jonah knew bears were fast. His mother was rarely worried about animals in the woods, but this was one for which she had a healthy respect. Jonah had seen pictures of people who had been mauled. Akilah motioned again, exasperated. He pointed to the ground, no.

Akilah stared fiercely. When he did not respond, she took a peek at the bear. Then she put her back to the embankment, away from the creature, and faced the boat. She tensed her arms.

Oh no you don't! Jonah yelled silently. Too late. She pushed off the slope, grabbed the lip of the boat with one hand and the paddles with the other. She ran for the water.

Jonah choked in disbelief. He looked over. The bear was standing, staring, moving. The growl from across the tundra shook his bones.

He reached for the seal, but his hands slipped uselessly off the skin. He grabbed the wood instead and ran for his life.

The bear charged. Akilah was already in the water. She waved frantically at him to hurry. With a clambering and scattering of loose rock, Jonah shot across the beach and into the water. The shore fell away and he was swimming, pushing the bundle of wood ahead of him. The bear crashed into the water. Jonah yelled, anticipating the tearing claws.

Akilah grabbed his hair. She hauled him up until he could leverage himself in. Jonah scrambled, using her arms to pull himself up. The bear remained in the shallows up to its forepaws, agitated and pacing, swinging its head back and forth. They watched the massive creature, both of them panting.

Jonah smacked the boat. "You left me back there!"

"I forced you to follow me."

"Same thing," he retorted. He was so angry he wanted to push her into the water. He punched the boat again. This time Akilah crossed the paddle over her chest. She glared at him.

He glared back.

The bear grunted loudly and then turned. It shook its head at both of them as if to say their argument was boring. *Come back here and talk to me about it, if it is worth the argument.* To emphasize the point, it lumbered down the beach, shaking its giant rump at the disagreeable creatures.

They followed his course and saw a herd of goats in the grass not far away.

"He has not smelled the seal," Akilah said.

The bear turned at her voice, grunted, then resumed his path.

Jonah shivered. The wind blew goose bumps into life. "Sorry. I should have followed you. I thought he was going to move on. I thought . . ."

"We have to light a fire and get warm. I hope there is enough dry wood." She nodded at the bundle of sticks floating in the water. "If not," she continued, "there are some trees over there, beyond the hollow of the tundra."

He noticed the copse of trees five hundred meters or so beyond where they had slept.

"Can we land? What about the bear?" he chattered.

Her gaze went to the animals on the tundra. "He has something new to hunt. Many more of them. And they are smaller than us. There will be a sick or young one among them. It will make a quick meal for the bear. There is also a large stream where the goats are feeding. "

Sure enough, the gray light shimmered on a river only a kilometer away.

"Will the bear come back?"

She shrugged. "How can we know? I think not likely. If we build a fire, the animals will stay back. I should have made one when we first landed, but I was tired and my shoulder hurt so much. Smoke travels far and they avoid it. But it can bring Crossers." She looked at the goose bumps flooding across his skin. "We need fire. Keep warm by paddling," she said.

He was grateful she had said "we," although she did not appear as cold as he felt. They pulled out the bundle of sticks on their way back to the shore, then dragged the boat back to the hollow. The bear was no longer in sight. Akilah took the wet skin from the sticks and squeezed much of the water out of it. Then she laid it on the ground. This time she placed the boat flat on the tundra instead of leaning it against the embankment.

She raised one end. "Get in."

Jonah hesitated. He remembered his foolishness of the previous night, but the sight of her standing there soaking wet and with her sore arm made him pause. "This is not like last night," he said. "I'm not as cold. And you are injured."

She thought for a moment. "You are the best one to paddle right now. We need you to be strong. I am not cold." She glanced around. "It does not harm me the way it does you."

"I noticed that," he answered. "You are acclimatized. Still, what about the bear? Better two of us take him on than one."

She smiled appreciatively. "I will watch."

"Akilah?"

"Yes."

"Will it take long to make a fire?"

"I do not know. The wood we brought is soaked. There may be dry grass under the pines."

"What if the bear comes?"

She sighed. "I can see everything that approaches from the pines." Then she added, "Besides, the running would warm you."

"That's not funny!" he said hoarsely. He watched her make for the pines. The grasses clung to the hem of her wrap as she walked. It was amazing how obviously her trail announced their presence. He would never have noticed it before. Now it stood out glaringly like a signal, like a signature in the grass.

Jonah raised the lip of the boat and ducked under. The wind was cut off, lessening the chill. He scrunched himself into the tightest ball he could and tried to control his shivering. He peeked out to watch her progress. Grass, sky, birds. Mountains in the distance, ocean. Nothing else. He stared for as long as his strength lasted. "I'm supposed to be taking care of her and here I am in the fetal position again!" Then he lowered the boat and closed himself into a miserable darkness.

* * *

Some time later he stirred.

"Jonah?"

"Hmmm?"

"Jonah!"

A roaring fire crackled at his feet. His face was warm and he was sitting on soft sand. Across from him, with her back against a giant log, was his mother. It was night.

He jerked forward. "Mom!" His heart raced and he looked wildly for Akilah. But the pines were gone. He could see the outline of the tents, exactly where he had re-set them. Bags of gear, his hiking boots, tackle box, it was all there. The moon was bright in a clear sky. He was aware of the overpowering smell of the forest. The scent of trees, bushes, shrubs, and mold was thicker than the fire smoke.

His mother took a sip from her mug. "You should go to your tent if you're tired."

"Mom," he stammered. "What am I . . . ? Where is . . . ?"

"Go to bed, Jonah. You're dreaming."

A little moan escaped his lips. His head pounded.

"You okay?"

He opened his palms. Warm, even sweaty.

There was no sign of Akilah. Waves of heat pushed against his chest and flowed across his shoulders, bringing with it the pungent smell of wood and leaves. The density of the forest was so pressing he felt claustrophobic. His eyes darted to his mother and he half expected her to disappear.

"Calm," he murmured. What had Akilah said? They were on a quest. Strange things happened on a quest. Another shift was happening. "Quest," he repeated. He glanced furtively for any sign of mist.

His mother watched him from over her mug. "You look a little disoriented, Jonah. Did you have a dream?"

With his heart still far from slowing down, he simply shook his head. How many times had he wanted to see his mother's familiar face in the last twenty-four hours? And now that she was here, or rather, now that he was back, all he could think of was Akilah.

"You look so much like your dad," his mother interrupted his thoughts.

"I do?" he stammered.

"Yeah, a lot. Although, sometimes you look like me, too."

"Mom," he whispered. The weight of everything he had experienced with Akilah crashed in on him. "I have to tell you.

You'll never believe it." He felt horribly awkward, as if he were about to give away a secret.

"Go to sleep!" she cut him off. "Forget it."

He frowned. She seemed completely unaware that he had been gone. "No. Mom . . . you'll never guess . . ."

She waved a hand. "For some reason I keep thinking about your dad. And you are no help. You do so many things the way he did. Some of them bug the heck out of me." One of the logs had fallen out from the fire circle and was not contributing to the flames. She kicked at it, sending a frenzy of sparks into the air.

Jonah stared. What was he supposed to do? A million things had happened and he was bursting to say them all. Why had she not noticed he was gone? And why had he come back? His thoughts pounded along with his heart. What would Akilah do?

Why must you know the answers before you walk the path? Her voice echoed in his mind.

His mother was still talking. "Did you know that he used to get mad when I forgot to clean the water pump? Of course you don't know that. And maps! Oh! He never looked at them."

Jonah took a deep breath. Thinking of Akilah, he faced the quest. "You need to forgive him, Mom. It wasn't his fault."

"Yes, it was!" The mug fell from her hands, spilling coffee onto her wrist and into the fire. "He could have died from a heart attack when he was eighty. Instead, he falls from a cliff and leaves me alone with a son who needs him as much as I do! Because he didn't read his map!"

The fire spat and whistled furiously.

Jonah swallowed. "He didn't do it on purpose. He—"

"It was stupid!" She concentrated on her wrist.

Silence.

"Stupid."

"Mom," Jonah said gently, "you would not have forgiven him if he had died from a heart attack, or cancer, or anything else beyond his control. You're just really sad that he's gone."

"I burned my hand."

"Don't worry so much about me, Mom. Akilah says . . . well, it's up to me now. I can make you guys proud."

"Who is Akilah?"

"Hmmm?"

She frowned. "You said, 'Akilah.'"

He cleared his throat. "No, I didn't. I said, 'Tequila.' I could use some."

She stared through him for the longest time. "Your dad was my best friend. And I'm terrified that you're going to disappear like him."

"I won't!" How could he explain? The surf crashed on the beach and he thought of Akilah. *You are here with me because you made a heart decision.*

"Mom. Sometimes it's good to make decisions with your heart, too. Even if it's risky."

She sniffed. "My hand, Jonah."

He lurched for the medical kit.

"Let me see it." He spread the ointment briskly. "No coverings on burns . . ."

"Unless they're deep," she finished.

Jonah examined her wrist. "Told you coffee was bad for you."

She nudged him. "Sit down. Thank you. You did a good job." She leaned against her log, closing her eyes. "It's this place, Jonah. Something about this trip."

"Yeah. I know," he agreed. "Feels like anything could happen."

"Something like that."

He waited, letting her settle while his own heart lunged with questing urgency. With all his being, he knew he had to go back to Akilah. He could not leave her until she was safe with her people. "Tell me about this place. Tell me everything. What was it like fourteen thousand years ago?"

"You were going on about that earlier," she smirked. "My son, the historian. What a nice change from fish."

"Tell me. I need . . . I really want to know."

She stretched her legs. "All right. What do you want, geography, flora, fauna . . . ?"

"Everything."

She took a deep breath. "Fourteen thousand years ago. We would be sitting on grassy tundra right now. The fire likely would not have been large because there wasn't as much wood. We have evidence of some scattered forests, not much variety that we know of . . ."

"Pines," Jonah interjected. "They are pines."

"They *were* pines. Very good, Jonah. How did you know that?"

"Tell me more."

She gave him a curious glance. "We think the tundra reached out really far in some places and almost connected the Charlottes to the mainland."

"But not here?" he asked.

"No." She eyed the coffee pot. "We know that because scientists found a certain kind of mollusk in this area."

Jonah shrugged and poured her another cup.

"Some things can't live where ice exists. So, if they find the shells in a certain place, it means that there wasn't any ice in the area at that time. Then they date the shells. In this area, where we are camping, they found the mollusks, dating back fourteen thousand years. In other words, no ice. We are sitting in an ancient, ice-free zone!"

Very good, Mom, Jonah thought. A short stab of pain at his temple made him flinch. He suddenly felt hot and his eyes suddenly bounced, heavy with sleep. Near the trees he sensed a haze, a mist flowing from between the trunks.

"What about animals?" he mumbled.

"Some, we think. Caribou, goats . . ."

"Goats," he muttered. "I've seen goats."

"Yes, yes, of course you have. And there were at least two kinds of bear, black and brown. They were likely the most dangerous creature at that time on the Charlottes. Not the largest, though. Many years before that, there were even mammoths."

"I haven't seen any mammoths," he said. It was so warm at the fire.

"What? No. The mammoths were long gone by fourteen thousand years ago, calendar time. Of course there were tons of birds, too. Cormorants, grebes, Common Muirs . . ."

His eyes were closing fast. "What about people, Mom? What about people?" His mouth felt full of marbles.

His mother's face blurred and wisps of cloud appeared, separating them, enclosing the fire.

"We don't know," he heard from a distance. "We haven't found anything much. The old coastlines are all under water. I think there were probably several groups from different parts of Europe and Asia . . . it's hard to know . . . harsh place back then . . . some groups probably survived. Some didn't. Some moved . . . wouldn't want to be alone out there . . ."

"No," he mumbled feverishly. "It's very tough. Akilah is tough. She shouldn't be alone out there. She shouldn't be there by herself. Not safe. I like her. I really like her. I'm doing my best, Mom. I'll do my best. We are on a quest."

* * *

"Jonah."

"Hmmm."

"Jonah."

He groaned. Something pressed against his lips.

"Drink this."

It was a shell. He opened his lips and water spilled into his mouth. It was a little briny, but otherwise soothing going down.

"Sit up."

He could not.

"Sit up."

She pulled at him.

The scent of grass and ocean replaced the wood smoke. He opened his eyes. He was leaning against Akilah with his back to her chest. He knew it was her—long strands of black hair swung past his cheek. The boat was no longer above him, and the grass bent with the wind all the way to the sea. He rested against her and allowed his eyes to close again.

"Wake," she commanded.

"No."

"Jonah, wake."

"No. I like this. And I keep going from place to place. I just want it to stop for a bit."

She sighed. "You have to get up. It is bad for you to sleep when you are cold. We should be moving. Back into the boat. We have to paddle to the hot springs before nightfall. It is the best chance of making you warm. And see, I have the seal skin. We will need to soak it in the spring."

"Too much effort. I am warm." He groaned as a memory suddenly tugged his thoughts. There was something he needed to tell Akilah. Something about being alone.

He felt her cold hand on his cheek. A second later she pressed her own cheek against his. "How did you become warm? I could not start the fire. And your wrap is no longer wet."

He nodded. "It was my mom. She built a huge fire. It was beautiful. And she told me about the tundra and the ice."

Akilah whirled around. "Where is she?"

"Not here," he answered. "Not yet. Not for many years." He looked at her, at the blowing grasses and the waiting sea. He shook his head in wonder. "Thanks for your words, Akilah. About quests, and about my dad. Whatever happens here, I will never see my old life the same way again."

She stood and offered him her hand.

"How is your shoulder?" he asked.

"It is still sore."

"Is it bleeding?"

"I do not know."

"Let me see."

He helped her slide her arm out. The rock had left an imprint of speckled blood spots. "It's healing," he observed. He touched the drying wound. "This is a harsh place. It isn't good for anyone to be alone out here. We have to find your people. Fast. I don't know when I'm going to be pulled away. Next time might be forever. We've got to get you back before that happens or you will be left alone out here."

She put her arms on top of his. "I am not alone."

"Yes, but for how long?" he urged. "What if I get taken before we find your people?"

"Why would you be pulled back before it is time?"

He shrugged. "Because it could happen. We don't know when the voice will strike again."

She laughed. "Your talk sounds like lightning."

"That is what it's like!" Jonah agreed.

She tugged on their overlapping arms. "How do your people live with no trust? We are here for a purpose. Both of us. Let us keep walking the path until our tasks are done."

He groaned. "We don't even know what that is."

"For now, it is to search for the People." She leaned her head toward him and their foreheads touched. "At least you no longer believe I am a dream."

Chapter Nine

Jonah turned the map upside down. "They aren't separate islands. They're all one."

"What is wrong?"

He pointed to the paper. "They are supposed to be individual islands. But they're not. See? House Island, Hot Spring Island . . . they are separate. Not here." He waved at the rising coast ahead. "It's like one piece of land. So, where does that put the hot springs?"

"Can you find it?" Akilah asked.

"I think I can get us to the right area. We might have to hunt a little."

She nodded.

Once again they were met by tundra at the shoreline. A small mountain was at its center, and Jonah figured it was the most likely place to find the hot springs.

"There are no tracks," she murmured. "There are caribou trails over there. But no people."

"They could have come a different way," Jonah suggested.

"Yes. So could the Crossers."

He cringed. "We have to hope they are in those mountains."

They walked side by side across the tundra. Akilah insisted that they dismantle the boat before starting up the slope of the mountains. "We must be ready to run with our hands free."

The hike would keep them busy enough, Jonah noted, and he

eyed the elevation change grimly. There was little cover. Anyone at the top had the distinct advantage. He clenched his fists. Whatever they met up there, he would stand beside her.

Jonah carried the new sealskin, still heavy and sagging. It smelled like fur and fish all at once.

"What are you going to do with it?" he wrinkled his nose.

Akilah turned constantly, searching and smelling.

Jonah fought off bugs, hundreds of them, leaping from the grasses in cohorts of biting troops. Tundra was like that. Sometimes bugs would drive animals insane. "We've got to move, Akilah. I hate these bugs! Why aren't they biting you?" he swiped at his face. "They all want me."

At the foot of the mountains she stopped walking. "There are more goats here," she pointed to a trail of broken stems leading into the heights. She sniffed and walked away from him.

At her feet was a large pile of bear stool. Jonah's heart thumped.

"It's old," she said. "The bear had a meal here." She pointed beyond the stool when Jonah could just make out a bundle of sticks poking up from the grass. They walked over. It was a rib cage.

Akilah poked at the grisly skull. "Caribou."

The bones were scattered, pulled away by animals, some as much as twenty meters. Not a piece of the skin or flesh was left. Jonah swallowed.

"Take this." Akilah handed him a femur the length of his arm. Jonah found the whiteness disturbing and far too human. "It is all we can carry," she said.

Her hands disappeared into the skeleton and she wrestled with something at its base. When she stood, she was holding a small, thin bone, more like a splinter than anything else. "Needle." She clenched it between her teeth, testing it, then placed it in her pouch.

He grimaced. "A needle? You rip a bone from an animal's body to sew on a patch, and I just throw my clothes out and buy new ones."

She pushed him playfully. "Walk. It will be dark soon."

"Can you teach me to sew?"

"Yes."

"My mom would love that. Shonika would laugh, but I don't care. I have a new respect for clothes."

"Jonah. We need to find a place to sleep."

"I don't want to sleep."

"Why?"

Hoisting the sealskin higher on his shoulder he replied, "Because I don't know where I'm going to wake up anymore. What if I wake up sitting across from my mom like the last time and can't get back? This place terrifies me but I'm not leaving you here alone!"

A warm wind blew at their backs as they scaled the heights, driving the bugs away. "Hallelujah!" Jonah sang. "Wind, the greatest bug-off!"

"Quiet, Jonah!" Akilah said. "The wind is blowing our scent to anyone or anything that waits at the top."

The rock was still warm despite the overcast sky, and the prospect of climbing was exhilarating. They exchanged smiles.

"Your father would like this?" Akilah asked.

"Definitely. And my mom would be so proud. I'm using my map every day!" The wind at his back felt like an encouraging pat from his parents, and his grin widened.

Akilah took the lead, hardly using her hands. Jonah followed each step and handhold. It was difficult moving with their burdens, and he found himself compensating, using more caution than usual. Although the drop was not severe, a fall would mean a painful roll down the slope. "Concentrate," he hissed to himself.

A second later Akilah slipped. A trickle of dust and stones rolled past. The boat skin and frame dangled near his nose. Jonah caught her foot and planted it firmly against the rock. "Got it?" he grunted.

She nodded gratefully. "The stones are so loose here."

Sweat trickled behind his ear. When the slope finally leveled off, he allowed himself a look around.

"Trees," Akilah announced proudly.

There were about twenty of them, short, no taller than his mother, with thick little branches. They could have been Christmas pines.

"Cute." He rubbed his fingers along the needles of a branch. He smelled his fingers. "Smells the same." Scooping up a fistful of dead needles, he panned the hilltop. "Not much of a forest, eh?"

Akilah touched a branch lovingly. "They are beautiful. And hard to find."

Jonah panned the islands around them. Tundra was the most obvious feature of everything he could see: tundra, rock, and ocean. There were pockets of green, likely more pines, but not a lot.

"One day," he swept his arm across the Charlottes, "this place will be filled with more trees than your eyes can handle. The land will smell of forest and moss and green things."

He watched her process the news.

"Your people must be very happy," she said.

He let the needles fall. "We're not very good with that sort of thing. That's why Mom and I came here. She's writing a story about how badly it has been treated. What do you call it, this place, anyway?"

She looked confused. "We call it the sea and the land."

He smirked. "Over time this place is going to be logged. We are going to cut the trees down in a way that will make you sick."

"Why would you do that?" she whispered and wrapped her arm around the closest trunk. Jonah stared at her dusky face, her caribou skin, the pouch at her waist filled with bone needles and stones, and herbs picked painstakingly from the world. He looked out at the ocean, at the tundra soon to be covered in water, and the land whose name would be known as a rainforest all over the globe. How could he answer? He needed pictures—from history and time and the ruin of many good things.

She put her arm around his shoulder, an ancient arm, young and strong and wise. "That is sad," she whispered. "Trees are beautiful."

"Yes, they are."

"Jonah. When you are taken back... you must be a rememberer! You must remind your people. Gather what you see here and remind them of what is good."

He shook his head sadly. "There are so many people in my world, Akilah. So many. My voice is drowned before I even open my mouth. And even if I did, there is little hope of anyone believing me. Not many people go on quests like you any more. Not where I live."

Akilah thought for a moment. "I remember for the People. I do not remember for the Crossers. How could I do that? You can only speak to whom you belong. You could start with your people."

"Good point."

She tugged his shoulder. "And you give me hope, Jonah. My heart smiles when I hear there are many people like mine in the years to come." She paused and then added, "Will you tell them about me?"

He considered. "I will. I have to. I want to."

Akilah nodded. "That is a beginning. Now you honor your father by telling the stories in his place. And you tell them with your heart!"

"Yep," he agreed. "But first we have to survive this path. Look at us! We're covered in bruises and cuts, and we haven't even found your people yet."

Akilah sniffed. "The hot springs are down there."

"Where?"

"Down there." She pointed to the slope ahead.

"How do you know?"

"The wind stopped and I can smell it."

"You can smell hot water?" he crinkled his nose.

"No. There is an odor from deep down under the ground."

Jonah hefted his burden. "What about these things?"

"Hide them," she answered. "We need our hands. We must come back the same way to get them."

They picked their way through the small pines to the inner mountain. Akilah stopped several times to collect more items for her pouch. Halfway down the slope they spotted the springs. Like giant teardrops, the hot pools leaked from one to another in a small cascade of steaming water. Steam poured off the surface, revealing only shapes through swirling mist. Jonah's aches and pains pulsed. They exchanged glances and quickened their pace.

Suddenly his back was pressed against the wall of the hill.

"Be silent!" Akilah hissed. She pointed with a shaking finger.

Amidst the swirling steam a figure stood and walked along the water's edge. He crouched and dipped his fingers. And then Jonah noticed the others. One, two, three, he counted at least a dozen more, male and female, lying around one of the lower pools. He wanted a better view.

She pressed back. "No."

"They are far away," he argued. "We can look."

She shook her head. "They will have watchers. And see . . . ?" She covered her mouth in horror.

Jonah stared. "What?!"

"Boats," she pointed. "They have boats."

Jonah's pulse picked up.

"We leave," Akilah whispered desperately. "Now!"

Turning on the hill was not as easy as going down. Jonah felt the earth give way beneath him, and a tumble of stones went down the slope. They froze.

"Go," Akilah urged.

There was little purpose in hesitating now. They had to get to the boat before they were seen. Jonah reached for a tuft of grass above his head. His eyes widened as a leather-clad foot suddenly stepped on his hand, crushing his fingers. Someone yelled, a harsh, guttural call that joined his own yelp of pain. A muscular figure towered over him and hefted a sharpened stick. Instinctively, Jonah gripped the man's foot with his opposite hand and yanked with all his strength. The man's leg shot out from beneath him and he fell onto the slope. Sliding past, he took a whack at Jonah's head. Then he grabbed at Akilah.

Her ankle wrenched out from the mountainside and she landed on her back with a sickening crash. Jonah heard her breath catch as she fell, tumbling and rolling with the Crosser. Beyond them, people rushed from the pools, shouting and fleeing for cover.

Jonah's cheek throbbed when he looked down to see his friend sliding, helplessly tangled with their attacker. "Akilah!" he screamed and launched himself from the slope.

His bottom hit the side of the hill and bounced him up to his feet again. He found himself running long, jolting strides, completely out of control. In seconds he had caught the tumbling pair, although he was somehow traveling backwards by the time he reached them.

The top of his head cracked against bone and he came to a stop. His eyes opened to find Akilah pressed into his chest with her legs stretched up the hill. Jonah was sitting on their attacker.

The shouting intensified.

"Akilah?"

Her nose was bleeding. Her eyes flickered open.

"Can you climb?" he asked.

She nodded. Using each other as a ladder, they untangled, and stood shakily, trying to hold their balance against the slope. The hot springs swarmed with shouting, pointing people. Children huddled against mothers, and two or three males climbed toward them. Sunlight glinted on polished weapons.

The man at their feet groaned. With his eyes closed he looked younger, perhaps only a few years older than the two of them. His hair, painstakingly braided, was coated in dust from the fall. Akilah pulled her knife and drew back, aiming for his neck.

Jonah grabbed her wrist. "What are you doing?"

"Let go."

The Crosser was writhing now, exposing his neck to her knife. "Don't!" Jonah pulled her and they stumbled, her knife swinging wildly past his eyes. A cloud of debris bounced down the hill. They clung to each other, struggling for balance, until Jonah threw his back firmly against the rock.

Akilah wrenched herself free. "Follow me!"

His chest heaving, Jonah panted, "Where are they?"

The shouting ceased. Instead, the only sound to be heard was the tinkling of tiny landslides made by dozens of angry men, making their way toward them up the slope. The women stood silently below, children in arms, watching their warriors hunt the enemy.

Chapter Ten

Jonah and Akilah attacked the hill. They scrambled and grabbed grass and roots, anything to reach the top. Akilah sobbed.

Their belongings lay where they had left them and they scooped them up. It was not as steep closer to the sea and Jonah took short, quick steps, trying hard not to slam into Akilah. They choked on their own dust clouds and gasped for breath. On reaching the tundra, Jonah gave a hoarse, triumphant shout.

Akilah threaded the boat frame while she ran, keeping the loose pieces clamped between her teeth. Jonah saw the skin catch the wind and blow the boat straight into her face. She tumbled, rolled, and shot back up, hardly missing a step.

"Elik!" she whimpered. "Where are you?" Although they had never met, Jonah chanted the same name, hoping beyond hope that he might turn up to save them.

At the water's edge, Akilah slid the remaining piece into place. One more strap to tie. Jonah held the boat steady.

"They're coming!" he urged. "Hurry up! Hurry up!"

"Throw it in!" Akilah gripped the frame. Like fishermen hurling a net, they tossed it into the sea and charged after it. The boat sagged with their weight, one side caving in completely, drowning the bottom with water.

"Get out!" Akilah yelled. "Get out, get out."

He swam free. The shouting grew louder, nearer. One figure

far outdistanced the others, and his braided ponytail bounced off his back with each leap down the slope. Jonah cringed when he recognized him. The young man no longer carried a club. It had rolled down the hill when they fell together. Now the Crosser moved like a lion, bounding down the hill with the stealth of a seasoned warrior. He would not need a weapon to drown them both in the sea.

Standing up to her waist in the shallows, Akilah watched him coming.

"What are you doing?" Jonah yelled.

"Throw me the caribou leg!" she shouted.

Jonah tossed the animal bone. The Crosser saw the weapon but did not check his speed.

Akilah closed one eye to aim. The femur caught the man in the chest, bone against bone, and he fell. Akilah climbed back into the boat.

"Out farther!" Jonah yelled. "I'll swim."

She paddled for deeper water. Jonah pushed off the shallow floor and began to swim, pushing the sealskin ahead of him.

"Wait!" he spluttered. "Too fast!"

Akilah stopped. She offered her paddle. "Slowly!" Her face contorted, holding back her sob. "Put the sealskin in first." She supported the sides.

Jonah followed instructions and rolled into the boat. They were drifting swiftly from shore. The Crossers gathered in a jostling group with more streaming from the hill. They picked up the young man from the beach. Grass and dirt covered half his face. He broke from their supporting hands, picked up a stone and hurled it. The enormous splash landed short of the boat. He roared a string of angry words. Jonah said nothing and watched them grow smaller with each paddle stroke.

Akilah's hands shook with pain. She stopped paddling to squeeze her leg.

"It's the salt!" Jonah croaked. Every cut he had received on the hillside burned from the salt water. She turned to expose a cut that began at her knee. Lifting the hem of her tunic, he saw that it traveled up her thigh to her hip. Fresh blood oozed out. She brought her knees to her chest and wept.

Jonah's cheek pulsed. He held his injured hand on his lap and bobbed in stunned silence.

When their crying eased, they began to inspect their wounds.

"I ache all over," Jonah groaned. He flicked away a tear. "I was so scared."

They stared knowingly, then clasped in a bear hug that nearly tipped the boat. "And me!" Akilah sobbed. They rode the ocean swells for some time, slowly moving farther from shore and danger. A tiny dust cloud revealed the Crossers were still pursuing.

Jonah looked out sometime later, his cheek still pressed against his friend's shoulder, and watched the ancient world flow past. Flocks of cormorants and grebes skimmed the surface with an aviator's precision. He sat numbly, only seeing, thinking, and breathing. Nothing ceased; animals grazed, flies swarmed, the wind blew, and the life of fourteen thousand years ago existed with or without them.

Between the gusts that took their boat farther down the coast, he could smell his own sweat. He could smell Akilah, too. He breathed deeply. The human smell was comforting and he did not wrinkle his nose.

"We need water," Akilah said.

And that is when they stopped.

They entered a kelp bed and the boat stuck fast amidst the tangle of slimy heads and tails. Jonah reached over the side. Lacy strings like giant lasagna noodles entwined his fingers.

"We're stuck," he announced. The shore was a hundred meters away with a football field of solid kelp bed in the way.

Akilah sighed.

"We are stuck," he said louder. Something snapped inside him. He faced the sky. "Good enough for you?" he roared. "We're bleeding; we're exhausted." He held his arms out wide. "We were nearly killed back there!" He pointed at Akilah. "Look at her. Do you see what has happened? Where are you? *Where—are—you?*"

Akilah slumped.

Jonah drew in a breath, primed for his next rant, when he noticed the open water. A path, clear of seaweed, wound its way to the near tundra.

Akilah sat up. "Thank you," she whispered and nodded to the heavens. She flipped her paddle, using the grip-end to pull them through the seaweed and toward clear water. "You need not pray so loud," she said practically. "But I thank you for thinking of me."

Jonah glanced at the sky a long moment. He searched the shore for movement and sniffed. "I wasn't expecting an answer so quickly."

"Caribou," Akilah said hoarsely.

A large herd, their coats blending perfectly with the tundra, stood at the water's edge. Their heads were cocked curiously, following the boat.

"Water," Akilah announced. She changed their direction.

As they approached, the herd bolted and trotted swiftly toward the slopes. Jonah tumbled out and waded to shore.

"Wait!" Akilah called. "Not here."

"Why?"

"The herd has stood in the water."

Caribou scat was everywhere. "Farther up, then?"

"Yes."

He heard Akilah throwing their paddles farther up the beach, away from the tide. "Jonah."

He turned.

Akilah limped after him.

"I'm sorry," he muttered. He hurried to her and offered his back. "Get on." He expected an argument but there was none.

Akilah climbed on. She laid her chin on his shoulder as would a small child with an older sibling.

"Fourteen thousand years," Jonah gasped. "And a piggyback is still a piggyback."

Twenty meters up the stream, he stopped and put her down. "You're not really heavy," he wheezed. "I'm just too tired and sore from everything else."

Akilah shook agitatedly. "It stings."

"You've got cuts on the inside of your knee, too. So every time you bend it's going to hurt. Don't walk too quickly."

They limped farther up the stream, turning at every sound. Jonah's peripheral vision caught every movement, from a bird's shadow to the grass bending in the wind. There was no hiding on this part of the island. The hills were farther back from the water, and there was little undulating ground in which to hide.

"I'm not sure where we are," he muttered. "I think this is part of Murchison Island. The tundra is connecting them all. It's not Ramsay Island. We floated north, not south."

"This will be good for water." Akilah stopped at a bend in the stream. The water poured from a cascade that gurgled deliciously into a pool. They fell into the streambed and drank.

"It's so good," he whispered.

"Cold," she added.

Jonah dipped his hand, allowing the water to numb his skin. Then he removed his wrap and began to wash his chest and back.

He plunged his head into the cataract. He shook his hair like a dog.

Akilah sat in the pool with her legs stretched out, watching him. She dipped her arms to soothe her scratched skin. She looked up as a flock of ducks flew past. "I would like to wash, too." She stared at her own wrap, then back to Jonah.

He nodded. "I'll go watch for Crossers."

He threw his soaking wrap on the ground and sat with his back to the pool. Other than the blowing grasses, there was silence. He heard Akilah's pouch hit the ground, then her clothes rustling. He concentrated on the tundra.

"Why were you going to kill that man, back there?"

There was considerable splashing from the pool. "I did not know if he had strength to follow us. If we tried to climb the hill, he would have been closer than the rest."

"So you were going to stick a knife into him?"

"What would you have done?" she shot back.

"I don't know," he stammered. "Maybe I would have kicked him or something. I wouldn't kill him."

"Kicking him would not stop him from getting up. He almost caught us again. If I had not hit him with the caribou leg . . ."

"Depends where you kick."

Jonah inspected his arms and noticed that his tan had deepened without burning. He glanced at the sky and shrugged. "Less UV's." He stretched his legs out. He had not worn sunscreen for two days, and much of that time had been on the water. "I'd be a raisin back home," he muttered.

"I did not hear you," Akilah said and sat next to him, her clothes back on and her face clear of tear stains and blood. Although she appeared calm, her eyes shifted to the tundra and hills.

"Maybe that was it," he said.

"I do not know your meaning."

"You were in shock . . . stunned. That's why you attacked the Crosser."

She shook her head. "If the Crosser was here right now, I would stick my knife into his heart."

Jonah pulled at the coarse grass. "Why are you so violent?"

"I do not understand."

"I don't understand how you can kill somebody!" he retorted. "I mean, I can see you rolling him farther down the hill or something. But the guy wasn't even moving. He may have been dead already. And you were going to slit his throat. *Slit his throat!*" Jonah slid his finger across his neck.

"He was not dead."

"Well, as good as dead."

Jonah stared at the trampled path of the caribou. "You are a wild animal sometimes," he whispered. "I do not understand you."

Akilah folded her arms across her knees. "And you, Jonah. You would be dead. You would have frozen the first night. And what about the bear? You say I am like an animal? Do you know what the animals are like? Do you know how they kill? Do you know how claws and teeth kill another slowly, with pain? I do not eat Crossers, Jonah. I am not an animal. I am one of the People."

Resting his head in his hands, Jonah groaned.

She stood. "I do not want to talk to you when you call me an animal. But I have to find the People."

He ripped a stem of grass unhappily. "There are a million places they could have gone. I'll have to guess."

"Make your choice."

"Fine, I will. We are going to Kunghit Island."

She nodded. "Then let us go. Remember, these new Crossers have boats, too. They will not stop hunting us. They will think we are bringing news to others. Their safety is in killing us. I can only pray the People are alive."

Hearing the worry in her voice, Jonah reached out and caught the edge of her collar as she turned to leave. She spun faster than he could react and brought her fist up under his chin. Her eyes blazed.

Jonah pointed his finger right between her eyes. "You see that? That's rage. That's what I'm talking about. You would probably even kill me. You're an uncivilized cave girl."

She snorted. "Your mother was correct. Your thoughts are unsteady. I would never kill you."

Jonah did not back down. "No one in *my* family has ever killed anyone."

She pushed his finger away. "No one in *my* family has ever had to take care of a twelve-year-old male because he could not survive on his own." Before he could say anything, she swung around and headed for the boats. "And I do not hate the Crossers. I fear them," she called over her shoulder. "They are like starvation in my stomach. If I kill a Crosser, it is so I can live. This is the way it has always been."

Only after she reached the boat did he follow.

Chapter Eleven

Jonah hugged his knees. They did not make a fire, as the danger of being discovered was too great. Added to their troubles was the fact that the Crossers had boats, as well. Jonah groaned. Akilah found the shallow cave only a few hundred meters down the coast, and they decided to stay the night rather than start the long trip to Kunghit Island. She threw herself into the boat and tried to sleep. Jonah took refuge at the entrance to gather his thoughts.

He hated the uncomfortable silence between them, but there was no easy way to make up. Whenever he closed his eyes, horrid, angry faces gnashed their teeth at him, and he envisioned himself wildly falling down the hill again. In the privacy of the cave mouth he had thrown up. Akilah was angry with him. He felt alone in a dangerous place and time that were not his own. "I don't know what to do," he whispered.

* * *

A brilliant sunset bathed the ancient world. The mountains were pillared against the darkening blue of encroaching nightfall. Here and there, mountain goats like tiny clouds moved on unseen trails. Below him, the tundra, billowing in restless golds and greens, was teeming with animals. The caribou herd headed back to the stream. The sea was alive with rolling swells and white-capped waves that crashed against the beachhead below. The air was clean and fresh and he inhaled deeply.

The wind had dried his clothes long ago. *A good thing*, he thought, for he sensed the bite in the air and knew the temperature would start dropping. He sniffed, raising his nose as Akilah did.

"How long have I been here?" he murmured. "Feels like months."

Akilah was in the boat and, other than the edge of her wrap sticking up above the side, he could not see her.

Don't put your arm around her, he told himself. *Snuggle in. Warm. No touching.* He closed his eyes. *Wait for the sun to go down.*

Jonah faced the wind. He remembered his mistake of staying out too long. "Stupid. That was stupid. Won't do that again." He looked back quickly to see if she heard. She was twitching, but nothing more. He shivered.

The first shooting star flared above the sea. "Where are you?" he said to the sky.

The shooting star brightened, right in front of him, before blowing itself out in a trail of celestial sparks. He stood and sighed. Beautiful. And completely out of control.

He froze in mid-thought and stared harder. He felt a presence in the coming twilight. Someone was there.

"Who is it?" Jonah trembled. He sank to the ground. His legs collapsed and his heart started thumping. *No one was there.*

And yet . . . there *was.*

He blinked. The stars had suddenly grown enormous, clustered, even overlapping in a cosmic race to his cave. Their brilliance lit up the islands and sea, and he covered his face with his arms. The cave floor pushed against him like a living thing and forced him to sit up. The air grew rich with the smells of evening grass, field flowers, and fresh earth, as if someone had picked a bouquet. The ocean roared below so loudly he covered his ears.

"*Someone* is coming," he gasped. "*Someone* is here."

A second later the sound of the ocean stopped. The light and air pulsated around him. Jonah held on, waiting for the walls to crumble. Shooting stars blazed like celebration fireworks.

"I am here," said the voice.

"I am afraid," Jonah whispered.

A gust of wind blew against him, bringing the fresh night air with increasing pungency. He raised himself to one knee. The wind gusted again, like an arm, supporting, lifting at his shoulders.

"That's a bit better," he gasped.

The wind blew stronger, warmer, tugging now at his arms and legs. Light and warmth filled the air and his limbs stopped shaking. He stood and faced the wind.

"I feel better now," he said. "Thank you."

Jonah could sense a crowd, not of people, but of everything around him, as if the earth were watching, aware of the visitor.

He listened to the stillness. As he stood before the voice, everything that had happened rushed through his mind, vividly, relived in a heartbeat.

Jonah waited breathlessly. He did not know where to look. The voice was not coming from the stars or the ocean or the rock. He felt a hundred emotions until they all settled on one. "I am sorry I hurt Akilah. She was right from the very start. She's not an animal. She's brilliant." The wind caressed his face.

Tears poured down his cheeks but he was not ashamed. "Why did you bring me here?"

The voice, when he heard it this time, was not one that resounded in his ears but spoke rather to his heart, like a familiar thought or smell, and vibrated through his bones. It was both deep and wild.

"Everyone is called to Quest."

Jonah then sat before the voice and thought for a long moment. He felt no urge to hurry. "I don't think I've met anyone who has gone on a quest. Except Akilah."

More shooting stars roared overhead. The voice rumbled. *"Seeing a quest and going on a quest are not the same."*

Jonah nodded. "I wasn't sure I wanted to come. I almost didn't. Akilah seemed so strange; my head hurt; Dad just died; Mom and I . . . it was all so crazy."

"Sometimes you are asked to make your most difficult choices when you feel the least ready to choose them. And then a Quest can begin."

Jonah frowned. "Do other people experience things like this? I mean, wouldn't I have heard about them?"

Something like a hum or rolling song began and the stars flared brightly. And then the voice spoke again. *"Will you remember when you have left this place? Will you believe?"*

Jonah thought of his mother, of Shonika, and Ben. How would he explain this to them? And yet, how could he not? Nothing could ever be the same again.

"I'll try. But it's so hard when I can't see or hear you all the time."

The voice answered, *"You have found me in the mist so that when you are back on your journey and clouds of many kinds appear, you will remember there is a path to follow. Remember."*

"I will. But, please, why now? Why with Akilah? She's from a long time ago."

"What is time to me?"

A sudden longing burst into Jonah's heart. "Will I see my father again?"

"In time. But it is your mother who needs you now."

Jonah thought of her sitting by the fire, so sad without his father. "Yes. She does need me."

The voice spoke one more time: *"Remember me."* The last word continued as the longest note of the deepest song he had ever heard. The voice was so close now, Jonah held his arms out for an embrace. Gradually, the breeze died at his feet. He reached out to catch the back of the wind as it left the cave. The note continued. Jonah sat for the longest time, listening until the note was so far away he could no longer hear it.

He was aware of the stars shining so loudly he could have sworn they were singing. The ground was still and the storm of shooting stars ceased. The ocean was quiet. He closed his eyes and sighed deeply, peacefully.

When he stirred again, he was lying in the boat. Akilah was only a hand's breadth away and they shared the same wrap. He leaned up on one arm and stared at the stars. The light and warmth were gone, and he could not sense anyone in the cave. He had no idea how he had come to be in the boat. He gently brushed Akilah's cheek with the side of his hand. She blinked and he brought his face close to hers.

"I'm sorry," he said. "I'm sorry I said terrible things about you."

Her eyes were full of question.

"You are not a cave girl. You're the smartest person I've ever met. And the prettiest."

She kissed him.

They both giggled.

Jonah lay down. "And I think I understand now why we are together. We both needed the right person for this quest. Time was in the way." He pulled the wrap tighter around his chin. "We have been given time together. I don't know for how long. But I'm so grateful for it."

She grabbed his hand. After a moment she said, "You give me hope, Jonah. For you have seen the time that is ahead. All my life I have feared that the People would starve or be killed by Crossers. When I look at you, I know I must continue searching. For you have seen us many years from now. And we are alive."

The night deepened as they slept. No bears or Crossers came near the cave, only the wind, as if on guard, blew steadily past the entrance until morning.

Chapter Twelve

"Wake up, Jonah."

He stirred, and with the movement felt every scrape and cut he had received the day before. "Ouch," he droned. Beyond her he could see blue sky.

"I hurt everywhere," he groaned again. But he felt different. He felt alive despite the healing wounds. He remembered what had happened in the night.

"Akilah," he whispered. "I saw . . . no, I met the . . . voice."

She nodded. "As did I."

"You did? But you were asleep."

She shook her head. "No. A vision."

He watched her curiously. When she did not say anything, he asked, "And . . .?"

She faced the entrance of the cave. "It is not proper to speak like this about a vision. An elder may ask. But you should not. There may be time ahead when I should say something, and I will." There was not the least bit of offence in her tone.

"I didn't know," he answered soberly. "I won't ask again. Can I ask how you feel, at least? That wasn't something that happens every day. And I'm going to burst. I have to talk about it in some way. Look at my hands! They're shaking just thinking about it."

She laughed.

"I feel strong!" he said and sat up straight. "I feel like I could pick up our boat and run to Khungit Island." Then he added, "With you in it!"

She laughed again. "That is the Maker's breath on you. I feel it, too."

Jonah stared at his shaking hands. "That's potent breath. Better than a lifetime of Mom's coffee. Taken all at once." He looked up at her, his face brightening. "You know what else? I'm not scared. I just realized how afraid I've been for this whole trip. Non-stop. Scared almost every minute." He paused and gave her a long stare. "In fact, I was scared before I entered the quest. I was scared the moment I found out my dad died, and I've been terrified ever since."

"Until now," Akilah finished.

"Until now," he answered. His smile faded. "To honor you, I won't say what I was told last night."

"That is wise," she said.

"But," he continued, "I can say what I was not told."

Her eyes widened.

"I was not told that the journey ahead would be easy. Or safe. It might even be the opposite." He thought of the stars that had blazed in the night and looked up to see the blue sky. Beyond the daylight, he knew, the stars still shone, hidden only for a time before their light would be made clear again by the darkness. "We have a path to follow," he said quietly. "Even if the way is not plain just yet. It will be."

Akilah reached out and took his hand. "You are a different Jonah than the one I first met."

He squeezed her hand. "I've had help."

The air smelled freshly clear of Crossers as they prepared to make their morning start. "How is your leg?" Jonah asked. She turned her leg over. There was still an ugly gash, although the jagged edges were closing.

Poking at the gathering scab, she shrugged. "I hope I do not have to run this day."

"I hope so, too," Jonah answered. "I am so thirsty. I could drink fifty of those shells."

"It rained in the early morning," Akilah answered. "There is good water everywhere. And the ocean is calm. We can paddle easily for a while before the wind grows stronger."

Jonah tapped the map. "Do you have any idea where we are supposed to look for the People?"

She shook her head.

There was a curious rock called All Alone Stone positioned three-quarters of the way south to Burnaby Island. They would use that as their guide across Juan Perez Sound.

They were cautious leaving the cave. It was a special place, and Akilah seemed grieved to leave. "Remember this cave, Jonah," she said and patted the entrance.

"I will never forget it," he replied soberly.

"You are getting darker," Akilah noticed as they climbed down the slope to the water. He looked at his arms. He always tanned well. However, this was deeper than anything he had experienced before.

She ruffled his hair. "Your hair is more yellow, too. It is almost white."

He smiled. "It does that every summer."

"You do not look strange to me anymore," she announced as they climbed into the boat.

They made excellent progress, working southwest toward the open waters of Hecate Strait. It was when they reached Ramsay that thc bubbling started.

"What is it?" Jonah asked nervously.

Akilah slowed. "A whale?"

"It's really bubbling." Jonah pointed. "Go around it."

Akilah jerked as she followed something beneath the surface.

"What is it?"

"Fish," she announced. "Hundreds of them. They are being chased by seals toward the shore."

The shiny bodies slid over one another in a frenzy. Fish smacked the underside of their boat as they moved into the bubbling zone. A dark shadow swam past.

"There's a seal!" Jonah pointed.

Akilah pulled off her belt. "Quick," she said. "There are many good fish. Give me the extra skin beside you."

Relieved it was only fish, Jonah turned to the seal pelt. He never reached it. A stick, longer than his leg, pierced the wall of their boat and stuck fast. Jonah stared uncomprehendingly. And then he heard shouts.

Akilah gripped the end of the spear. She pushed until it slid out. "Paddle!"

One glance behind revealed a boat with two Crossers. Only the rolling swells had kept the spear from piercing one of their hearts.

"Where did they come from?" Jonah shouted hoarsely.

"Paddle!" Akilah commanded again. They made for open sea.

"Where?" she asked a moment later.

"All Alone Stone!" he panted. "The land ahead."

"Too far," Akilah gasped.

"They are really close!" Jonah yelled. "Akilah, they are close!"

Her shoulders slumped. She exhaled and stopped paddling.

"What are you doing?" he yelled.

She dropped her paddle. Taking off her tool pouch, she tossed it at Jonah's feet. She grabbed his head, forcing him to look into her eyes.

"We have to upset their boat. I do not think they can swim. We can. It is our only chance." She released him. Without another word, she dove into the water. The boat wobbled dangerously and the sides sank low to the surface. He was alone. He could see her swimming back toward the oncoming Crossers. One of them reversed his paddle to hold it like a club.

The boat lulled. Ahead, All Alone Stone calmly reflected its tide-washed rock in the afternoon sun. It looked peaceful there. The boat rocked gently.

He groaned and threw down his paddle. "Why does she always run the wrong way?" Cursing, he curled his fists into tight balls and pushed his knuckles against his teeth. "This is it! This is it. Come on, Jonah!" He ripped off his skin wrap and stood with his feet spread wide. He jumped. The bottom sagged from his launch but he cleared the skin sides and entered the water. Bubbles and murk flowed past as he searched for the surface. The moment his head popped up, he plunged after Akilah.

The Crossers were uneasy. They talked back and forth as Akilah approached. Jonah saw one of them flip his paddle and brandish it, but he could tell they were nervous.

"Akilah, wait!" he coughed. The Crossers' balance was terrible and he was a little surprised they had ventured so far from land. Akilah had almost reached them. *They have used up their spear*, he told himself. He sucked in a breath when the blade brushed past her head. She submerged and pushed at the side of their boat, then tugged at it.

"Human torpedo!" Jonah muttered. "And an idiot! This is suicide."

The men shouted and whacked at the water. Jonah swam so quickly that when he looked up he hit the boat. Both men were busy with Akilah on the opposite side and did not notice him. He went under. Pushing against the men's weight, he could feel them lose balance. Then he lost his air and surfaced.

He saw the paddle coming and launched backward. The blade struck the water. One Crosser raised himself to his knees, ready to whack again. Suddenly the back of their small boat caved in. Jonah saw Akilah's small arm inside, heaving down on the bone frame.

Both men shouted. Akilah disappeared. They held their paddles high, searching and trying to control the waffling boat.

They were so close Jonah could see the spit of exertion on their lips. Frustrated, they splashed at him when he slipped out of reach.

It was a mistake.

Jonah caught a paddle and pulled. He felt the man lose his balance; then he swam to the opposite side. With a cry the man fell into the water. His leg was hooked to the boat, and while his partner tried to release him, the skin side dipped. Both men were in the water and, from their shouting, he gathered they were terrified.

Without the weight, Akilah easily pulled the side down and flooded the bottom. The Crossers yelled, splashed, and madly tried to stay afloat.

Jonah and Akilah swam away. Their own boat seemed distant, a bobbing brownish-gray spot. Jonah's sloppy strokes were losing power. "Stay calm," he sputtered when a wave caught him in the mouth. He slowed and flipped onto his back.

"Jonah. You are almost there," Akilah said. A moment later she added, "Here it is." She placed his hands on the skin sides.

At last they lay on the bottom, sucking air. They stayed there for some time, taking warmth from each other.

"They gone?" Jonah puffed.

She raised herself. "They are still struggling. One of them is in the boat. They are trying to get the water out. They will not chase us, I think. I cannot see their paddles." She nudged him. "I am proud of you. You grabbed his paddle. I could not reach it."

He managed a grin.

They untangled and sat up. Fifty meters away, a Crosser swiftly bailed the boat with his hands.

"The other one is in now, too," he observed.

"Yes. It will take time to clear it of water." She gazed for a long time at the men. "Where are the others?" she mumbled.

"What others?"

"They would have sent more."

"Why do you say that?"

"Do you see how they keep looking back?"

He nodded. "Yes."

"They do this because they know there are others. They must have split their group to go around the islands. Or there are more coming behind them. I think they are not alone, Jonah."

Jonah looked the other way. The afternoon sun had come out and bathed them deliciously. He licked his lips. Then he took hold of his paddle and said, "All Alone Stone. There is tundra around it as well. Not much of it, but at least bigger than in my time. I am so thirsty."

"We must gain more distance."

"We're still alive," Jonah sang. "We're still alive." The temptation to look behind every few seconds was overwhelming.

"The sun is hiding their progress," she answered. "I see movement, but that is all. It is difficult to tell if they are even following. No, wait!" Jonah stared with her. The paddle splashes were unmistakable.

More small boats were crossing from Ramsay Island and heading right toward them. Although it was still far off, they could hear the rhythmic chanting of the paddlers.

"All Alone Stone," Jonah croaked hoarsely. "There is a strait, Burnaby Strait, just south of it. If the Dolomite Narrows exist, we might be able to lose them in there. It's a long way! But it's all I can remember."

On the map, the ocean channeled at one point, splitting Burnaby Island. All Jonah cared about was that the channel gave them an escape route, or at least a place to hide.

The afternoon wind hurried their little craft along.

"Halfway!" Jonah shouted. He could see bare rock with only scant vegetation. His heart sank. All Alone Stone offered no refuge for them despite its increased size. They passed it and stared hopefully at the rising mountains.

The Crossers shortened the distance.

Beside him, Akilah sucked back a sob and paddled harder. "We cannot tip ten boats," she gasped. "We have to make it to land. There may be a place to hide."

Sweat poured. The glare off the water was fiercely bright, but Jonah hardly noticed.

"What is that?" Akilah puffed. The land ahead was barren of trees and its bald head was crowned with short bushes and tundra, flowing from the mountain's feet. Yet far more important to their tired muscles was the narrow chasm that split the land in two.

"That's it!" Jonah croaked. "The gap between the rocks."

Their boat swerved in the new direction.

"Soon they will throw their weapons," Akilah said between breaths. "We are still too far from shore."

He could hear the splash of their pursuers' paddles, and with the sound came the whisper of death. The last vestiges of his courage failed. They were not going to make it. He slowed his strokes and bowed his head. There was no hope left. Nothing ahead. Only blind terror.

A booming sound made him look up. At the head of the tunnel, water sprayed high against the rocks with each surge of waves, and the near shore was dowsed in a fine mist.

"Mist," Jonah gasped.

Remember me.

"Paddle!" Akilah yelled.

Leaning forward, Jonah pumped with every last ounce of strength he had. His throat was as dry as the dust in the empty cave.

A large stone whizzed past Akilah's cheek. Another followed. They both looked back. Three boats had taken the lead and it was from them that the stones had come. The tundra was cut cleanly in half by the narrows, and Akilah had to work hard to keep their bow aimed for the opening.

The narrows came up quickly.

"Too fast!" Jonah croaked.

Skillfully, she guided them into the narrows. The water roared in surges against the walls. Water blasts fired shadows and echoes high around them as if they were being swallowed by the island's throat. Yet far more alarming were the several figures that stood on the walls of the channel, armed with bows and clubs.

"It's a trap!" Jonah yelled. "They set a trap!"